The Juniper Tree

THE JUNIPER TREE
and Other Tales from Grimm

Selected by Lore Segal and Maurice Sendak

Translated by Lore Segal
With four tales translated by Randall Jarrell

Pictures by Maurice Sendak

· II ·

Farrar, Straus and Giroux · New York

The Tales

The Pictures

VOLUME II

The Juniper Tree

The Frog King, or Iron Henry

In the old days, when wishing still helped, there lived a king and all his daughters were beautiful, but the youngest was so beautiful that even the sun, which has seen so much, marveled every time it shone into her face. Near the king's castle lay a great, dark forest and in the forest, under an old linden tree, there stood a well. Now on the days when it was very hot the princess would go out into the forest and sit at the edge of the cool well and if time hung heavy on her hands she took a golden ball, threw it in the air, and caught it, and it was her favorite plaything.

It happened once that the princess's golden ball did not fall into her outstretched hand but slipped past, struck the ground, made straight for the water, and rolled in. The princess followed it with her eyes but the ball disappeared, and the well was deep, so deep that you couldn't see the bottom, and she began to cry and kept crying louder and louder and could not stop. And as she sat wailing, someone called, "What's the matter, Princess? The way you howl would melt the heart of a stone!" The princess looked around to see who it could be and saw a frog sticking his thick, ugly head out of the water. "Oh, it's you, you old puddle-splasher," said she. "I'm crying because my golden ball has fallen into the well." "Well, don't cry any more," answered the frog, "I can help you. What will you give me if I bring back your toy?" "Anything you want, dear frog," said she, "my dresses, my pearls and all my jewels, and the gold crown on my head as well." "I don't care anything about your dresses, your pearls and jewels, or your golden crown, but if you will promise to love me best and play with me, and let me be your dearest friend, and sit beside you at the table, eat off your golden plate, drink from your cup, and sleep in your bed with you, I will climb down and bring back your golden ball." "Yes, yes, I promise everything, only bring me my ball," said she, thinking, The silly frog! What nonsense he does talk; he sits here in the water with his own kind and croaks, and can never be friends with real people.

When the frog had obtained her promise, he put his head in the water, sank down, and after a little while came paddling back up with the ball in his mouth and threw it on the grass. The princess was overjoyed to see her pretty toy, picked it up, and ran away. "Wait for me, wait for me," cried the frog. "Take me with you, I can't run so fast," but what was the good of his croaking after her as loud as he could? She would not hear him but hurried home and soon forgot the poor frog, who had to climb back into his well.

The next day, as she was sitting at the table with the king and all the court, and was eating from her golden plate, there came something crawling, splash, splash, up the marble stair. When it arrived at the top, it knocked and cried, "Princess, youngest princess, open the door." She ran to see who it was, but when she opened the door, there sat the frog. She quickly slammed the door, came back, and sat down, but she was in a great fright. The king could see how her heart was beating, and said, "Why are you afraid, my child? Is there a giant at the door maybe, come to carry you away?" "Oh, no," she answered, "it's not a giant, only a nasty frog." "What does the frog want with you?" "Ah, dear Father, in the forest yesterday I was sitting by the well, playing, and my golden ball fell in the water. And because I was crying so hard, the frog went and fetched it up for me, and made me promise that he could be my best friend, but I never, never thought he'd get out of his water, and now he's here and wants to come inside with me." At that moment there was more knocking and a voice cried:

> "Princess, youngest princess,
> open the door,
> don't you know what you

172

The Frog King, or Iron Henry

said to me yesterday
by the cool well-water?
Princess, youngest princess,
open the door."

Then the king said, "If you made a promise, you must keep it. Go, open the door for him." The princess went and opened the door and the frog hopped in, following her every footstep right up to her chair, and sat there and cried, "Lift me up where you are." She hesitated until finally the king commanded it. When the frog was on her chair, he wanted to be up on the table, and when he sat on the table he said, "Now push your golden plate nearer, so we can eat together." She did, but one could tell she did not like it. The frog ate heartily, but as for her, every bite stuck in her throat. Finally he said, "I have eaten till I am full, and now I'm tired. Carry me to your room and make up your silken bed so we can lie down and go to sleep." The princess began to cry. She was afraid of the cold frog, whom she could not bear to touch and who wanted to sleep in her nice clean bed. But the king got angry and said, "If someone helps you in your need, you must not look down on him afterwards." And so she took hold of the frog with two fingers, carried him upstairs, and set him in a corner, but when she was lying in bed he came crawling and said, "I'm tired too and want to sleep comfortably just like you. Lift me up, or I'll tell your father." Now this gets her really angry! She picked him up and she threw him against the wall as hard as she could: "Now will you be satisfied, you nasty frog!"

As he fell to the ground, however, he was no longer a frog but a prince with kind and beautiful eyes who, by her father's wishes, now became her friend and husband. And he told her how a wicked witch had put a spell on him and how nobody had been able to set him free from the well but she alone, and tomorrow they would go to his kingdom together. Then they went to sleep and next morning, when the sun woke them, a coach came driving up with eight white horses that had white ostrich feathers on their heads, all harnessed in golden chains, and in the back stood the young king's servant and it was his faithful Henry. Faithful Henry had been so grieved when his master was

changed into a frog that he had three iron bands laid around his heart to keep it from bursting with pain and sorrow. And the coach had come to fetch the young king home to his kingdom. Faithful Henry set them both inside and went and stood in the back and was overjoyed that his master had been freed. And when they had gone a little way, the prince heard a cracking behind him as if something had broken in two. He turned and cried:

"Henry, the carriage breaks apart."
"No, sire, it's not the carriage breaking,
it's the iron band around my heart—
my heart that lay so sorely aching
while you were a frog, while you sat in the well."

Again, and once again, as they drove along, came the cracking sound, and each time the prince thought the coach was breaking apart but it was only another band bursting from around the heart of his faithful Henry because his master was free and happy.

The Poor Miller's Boy
and the Little Cat

In a mill lived an old miller who had neither wife nor children, and three young fellows worked for him. One day when they had been with him for some years, he said, "I am getting old; I want to sit behind the oven and take my ease. Go out into the world, and whichever one brings home the best horse shall have the mill and in return he must take care of me until I die." Now the third young boy was only an apprentice. The two others took him for a simpleton and begrudged him the mill, though as it turned out in the end he didn't even want it. So the three of them set out, and as they were leaving the village, the two said to simple John, "You might just as well stay here, *you'll* never get a horse as long as you live." But John went along anyway and at nightfall they came to a cave and went in and lay down to sleep. The two smart ones waited till John had fallen asleep, then they got up and made off and left Johnny lying there and thought they had done something very clever; oh, but it won't do you a bit of good! When the sun came up, John woke and there he lay deep in a cave. He peered all around and cried, "Dear God! Where am I!" and he rose and scrambled out of the cave and went into the forest and thought, Here I am, alone and forsaken. How shall I ever get a horse! And as he was walking along deep in thought he met a little speckled cat that spoke kindly to him and said, "Where are you off to, John?" "Oh, it's nothing you can help me with." "I know very well what it is you want," said the little cat. "You want a pretty horse. Come with me and be my faithful servant for seven years and I will give you one more handsome than anything

179

you've seen in your whole life." What a strange cat, thought John, but I might as well go along and see if she is telling the truth. And so she took him with her to her bewitched little palace where she had nothing but cats to wait on her. They leaped nimbly up and down the stairs, happy and full of fun. In the evening, when they sat down to supper, there were three who made music; one played the double bass, another the violin, and the third put the trumpet to her mouth and blew up her cheeks for all she was worth. When they had eaten, the table was removed and the cat said, "Come, John, dance with me." "No," said he, "I don't dance with pussycats. That's something I have never done." "Then take him up to bed," she said to the little cats. So then one lighted him to his bedroom, one took off his shoes, one his stockings, and finally one blew out his candle. The next morning they came back and helped him out of bed; one put on his stockings, one tied his garters, one fetched his shoes, one washed him, and one dried his face with her tail. "That feels nice and soft," said John. John himself had to wait on the cat. Every day he had to chop firewood and had

180

a silver ax to do it with, and the wedges and the saw were all made of silver and the mallet was of copper. Well, and so he chopped and chopped and stayed in that house, had plenty of food and drink but never saw a soul except the speckled cat and her household. One day she said, "Go and mow the meadow and dry the hay," and she gave him a silver scythe and a golden whetstone and told him to be sure to bring everything back, and so John went and did as he was told and when he was finished he brought scythe, whetstone, and hay back home and said wasn't she going to give him his earnings. "No," said the cat, "first you must do one more thing. Here is silver lumber, and the carpenter's ax, the square, and everything you need all made of silver. Build me a little house with it." Well, and so John built the little house and when it was finished he said now he had done everything and still he didn't have a horse. And yet the seven years had passed as if they were six months. The cat asked him if he wouldn't like to see her horses. "Yes," said John, so she opened the little house and as she is opening up the door there are these twelve horses standing

183

there and oh, weren't they proud-looking, and didn't they shine and gleam like mirrors, it made his heart leap for joy. So then she gave him food and drink and said, "Go home. I won't give you your horse to take with you. In three days I will come and bring it after you." So then John got ready to leave and she showed him the way to the mill. But she hadn't even given him a new suit of clothes and he had to wear the old ragged smock he came in that had grown too short and tight for him in those seven years. Now when he got home, the two others were back as well, and though they had each brought a horse, the horse of one was blind and the other's horse was lame. They asked, "John, where's your horse?" "It's being sent after me in three days." They laughed and said, "Yes, John. Sure, John! Where would *you* get a horse? This is going to be something!" John came inside but the miller said they couldn't have him sitting at the table, he was so torn and ragged one would be ashamed if somebody dropped in, so they gave him a little bit of food to take outside; and in the evening, when they lay down to sleep, the two others would not let him in the bed, and he had to crawl into the goose pen and lie down on a little hard straw. And in the morning he wakes up and the three days have already passed and here comes a carriage drawn by six horses; my, it was a pleasure to see how they gleamed, and there's this servant and he's brought yet a seventh horse, which is for the poor miller's apprentice. But out of the carriage there stepped this magnificent princess and she came into the mill and the princess was the little speckled cat that poor John had served for seven years. She asked the miller where's the boy, the miller's apprentice? So then the miller says, "We couldn't have him in the mill he's so ragged, he's lying outside in the goose pen." So then the princess said they should go and get him at once. Well, so they went and got him out and he had to hold his little smock together to cover himself. And the servant unpacked magnificent clothes and washed him and dressed him, and when he was ready no king could have been more handsome. After that the lady asked to see the horses which the others had brought and one horse was blind and the other lame. So then she had the servant bring the seventh horse. When the miller saw it, he said that nothing like it had ever entered his yard. "Well, this is for the apprentice," said she. "Then he shall have the mill," said the miller, but the princess said he could have the horse and he could keep his mill and takes her faithful John and puts him in the carriage and drives off with him. And they drive to the little house he built with the silver tools and it is a great palace and everything in it is silver and gold and she marries him and he is rich—so rich he had plenty of everything as long as he lived. And that is why nobody should say that a simple person can never amount to anything.

Frederick and His Katelizabeth

There was a man called Frederick and a woman called Katelizabeth, and they got married and set up house together. One day Frederick said, "Katelizabeth, I'm going into the fields, and when I get back, you're to have a hot meal ready on the table for me and a cold drink to go with it." "Just you go along, Freddy dear," answered his Katelizabeth, "and you will see how nicely I will manage everything." Now when lunchtime drew near, she fetched a sausage out of the chimney, laid it in a frying pan, put in some butter,

187

and set it on the fire. The sausage began to cook and
sizzle; Katelizabeth stood by and held the pan handle
and thought thoughts, when it came to her: "While the
sausage is cooking, why couldn't you be drawing the
drink in the cellar?" And so she steadied the pan
handle, fetched a jug, and went down into the cellar
to draw beer. The beer ran into the jug; Katelizabeth
watched it running, when it came to her: "Hey! The
dog upstairs isn't chained and might steal the sausage
out of the pan. That's all I need!" One, two, up the
cellar steps, but the mutt already had the sausage in
his mouth, trailing it behind him as he ran. Katelizabeth, no slouch, made after him and chased him a good
way into the fields, but the dog was faster than
Katelizabeth and never let go, and the sausage went
skipping over the furrows. "Gone is gone," said
Katelizabeth and she turned around and, because she
was tired out from so much running, walked nice
and slow, to cool off. All this time the beer was running out of the barrel because Katelizabeth had not
turned the tap off, and when the jug was full and there
was nowhere else for the beer to run, it ran all over the

cellar floor and didn't stop until the whole barrel was empty. Katelizabeth saw the disaster from the steps. "Oh, hang," she said, "now what are you going to do so Frederick won't notice?" She thought awhile and in the end it came to her: they still had one sack of the beautiful wheat flour from the last church fair up in the loft; she could fetch it down and sprinkle it on the beer. "Yes indeed," said she. "Who saves in his day of plenty has in his day of need," and she climbed into the loft, carried down the sack, and threw it right on top of the full jug so that it overturned and Frederick's beer swam around the cellar too. "And quite right," said Katelizabeth. "Where one goes is where the rest should go as well," and she sprinkled the flour all over the cellar. When it was finished she was pleased with herself and said, "My, how neat and clean it looks!"

At lunchtime Frederick came home. "Well, wife, and what have you got for my lunch?" "Well, you see, Freddy," she answered, "I was going to fry you a sausage, but while I was drawing beer the dog stole it out of the pan, and while I was chasing the dog all the beer ran out, and when I wanted to soak up the beer with the wheat flour I knocked the jug over too, but don't you worry, the cellar is all nice and dry again." Said Frederick, "Katelizabeth, you shouldn't have done that! Let the dog steal the sausage and the beer run out of the barrel and pour out all our fine wheat flour too!" "Oh, but Freddy, I didn't know. You might have told me."

The man thought: "If that's the sort of wife you've got, you'll have to watch out." Now he had managed to save up a nice pile of thalers and he went and changed them into gold and said to Katelizabeth, "See these yellow chips? I'm going to put them in a pot and bury them in the cow shed, under the manger, but don't you go near them or there'll be trouble!" Said she, "Oh, all right, Freddy. I won't, I promise." Now when Frederick was gone, some peddlers came into the village selling earthen pots and pans and called at the young woman's house to ask if she would give them some business. "Ah, dear good people," said Katelizabeth, "I haven't got any money so I can't buy anything, but if you can use yellow chips, I could buy something." "Yellow chips—and why not? Let's have a look at them." "Go into the cow shed and dig under the manger, you'll find yellow chips; I'm not allowed to go near them." The rascals went and dug, found pure gold, and made off with it, leaving all their pots and pans standing around the house. Katelizabeth thought she ought to make some use of the new crockery, but as there was already plenty of everything in her kitchen she knocked the bottom out of every last pot and stuck them on the slats of the fence all the way around the house. When Frederick came home and saw the new decoration, he said, "Katelizabeth, what have you done!" "Bought them, Freddy dear, with the yellow chips from under the manger. But I never went near them myself. The peddlers had to dig it out for themselves." "Ah, wife," said Frederick, "now look what you've done! Those weren't chips but pure gold and it was our whole fortune. You shouldn't have done that." "But Freddy," answered she, "I didn't know. You should have told me."

Katelizabeth stood and thought awhile and then she said, "Listen, Freddy, we'll get the gold back all right. Let's run after those thieves." "Come on, then," said

Frederick, "we'll have a try. You bring along some butter and cheese so we'll have something to eat on the way." "Oh, all right, Freddy, I certainly will." They started on their way, and because Frederick was the better walker, Katelizabeth came along behind. "Which is all to the good," said she, "because when we turn back I'll be that much farther ahead." Now she came to a mountain where there were deep wagon ruts on either side of the path. "Will you look at that," said Katelizabeth. "How they've worn down and torn up and squashed this poor earth. It'll never heal as long as it lives." And out of the goodness of her heart she took the butter and smeared it on the ruts, right and left, so the wheels would not hurt it anymore. And as she stood bent over in her charitable act, one of the cheeses rolled out of her pocket and down the mountain. Said Katelizabeth, "I've made my way up once already, I'm not about to walk down again; let someone else go and bring it back," so she took another cheese and rolled it down the mountain, but the cheeses didn't come back, so she sent a third one down, thinking: "They're waiting for company, maybe they don't like walking by themselves." But when all three of them stayed down there, she said, "I don't know what to make of it, and yet it could be the third one didn't find its way and got lost. I might as well send the fourth down to look for them." But the fourth did no better than the third and so Katelizabeth got cross and threw the fifth and sixth down too, and they were the last. For a while she stood and listened but they would not and would not come, so she said: "You'd be the right ones to send looking for death, you take such an everlasting time. You think I'm going to stand around here waiting for you? I'll go about my business and you can run after me, your legs are younger than mine." Katelizabeth walked off and found Frederick, who had stopped to wait because he felt like having something to eat. "All right, let's have what you brought with you." She handed him the dry bread. "Where is the butter and cheese?" asked the man. "Well, you see, Freddy," said Katelizabeth, "the butter I smeared on the wagon ruts and the cheeses will be here soon. One of them ran away, so I sent the others to go and bring it back." Said Frederick, "You shouldn't have done that, Katelizabeth, smear the butter all over the road and roll the cheeses down the mountain." "Well then, Freddy, you should have told me."

So together they ate the dry bread and Frederick said, "Katelizabeth, and did you lock up the house before you left?" "No, Freddy. You should have told me." "So run back home and take care of the door before we go any farther. And bring something else to eat. I'll wait here." Katelizabeth went home and thought, "Freddy wants something else to eat; he probably doesn't like butter and cheese, so I'll wrap some prunes in a cloth and take along a jug of vinegar to drink." Then she bolted the top part of the door, but the bottom half she lifted off the hinges and onto her shoulders, thinking that if she took care of the door, the house would be safe. Kateliza-beth took her time on the way, thinking: "All the more time for dear Frederick to rest up." When she got back to him she said, "Here you are, Freddy dear. Here's the front door so you can look after the house yourself." "Good heavens," said he, "what a clever wife! Takes the bottom door off the hinges, so anybody can run in, and bolts the top! It's too late now to go home again, but since you brought the door this far, you can carry it the rest of the way." "The door I'll carry, Freddy, but the prunes and the vinegar are getting too heavy: I'll hang them on the door. Let the door carry them."

Now they went into the forest looking for those rascals, but couldn't find them. Finally, when it was getting dark, they climbed into a tree where they meant to spend the night; but hardly had they got to the top and settled down when along came those fellows who carry away what doesn't come of its own accord and find things before they're lost, and sat down under the very tree in which Frederick and Katelizabeth were hiding, made themselves a fire, and got ready to divide up the loot. Frederick climbed down the other side, gathered stones, climbed back with them, and was going to stone the thieves to death. But the stones did not hit and the rascals said, "It will be morning soon; the wind is knocking the pine cones down." Katelizabeth was still carrying the door, and because its weight was pressing into her back, she thought it must be the prunes and said, "Dear Freddy, I've got to throw down the prunes." "No, Katelizabeth, not now," answered he, "the prunes

195

might give us away." "Oh, but Freddy, I've got to, they're hurting me!" "Oh, all right, hang it, go ahead then." And so the prunes rolled down between the branches and the men below said, "It's bird droppings." A little while later, because the door was still pressing into her back, Katelizabeth said, "Dear Freddy, I've got to pour the vinegar out." "No, Katelizabeth, you mustn't do that, it might give us away." "Oh, but dear Freddy, I've just got to, it's hurting me so." "Oh, all right, hang it, go ahead then." And so she poured the vinegar out and it splattered the men below. They said to one another, "It's the dew already falling." Finally Katelizabeth thought, "Could it be the door digging into my back?" and said, "Freddy, I've got to throw the door down." "No, Katelizabeth, not now, it might give us away." "Oh, but Freddy, I've just got to, it's hurting too much!" "No, Katelizabeth, hold on tight!" "Oh dear, Freddy, I'm letting go." "Let it go then," answered Freddy angrily, "and the devil take it," and so the door fell down with such a clatter and the men below cried, "It's the devil coming down the tree," and bolted, leaving everything behind them. Early in

the morning, when the two climbed down, they found all their gold and carried it back home.

At home Frederick said, "Katelizabeth, now you must be a good girl and work hard." "Oh, I will, Freddy, I certainly will. I'll go out into the fields and mow the hay." Out in the fields Katelizabeth asked herself: "Shall I eat before I mow or shall I sleep before I mow? I know what, I'll eat first." And so Katelizabeth ate, and eating made her sleepy and she began to mow half in a dream and mowed her clothes in half, apron, skirt, and shirt. When Katelizabeth woke after a long sleep, there she was half naked and said to herself: "Is it me or isn't it? Aw, this is not me!" Meanwhile, night had come and so Katelizabeth ran into the village, knocked at her husband's window, and cried, "Freddy!" "What is it?" "I just wanted to see if Katelizabeth is in." "Sure," answered Frederick, "she's inside, lying down asleep." "Fine," said she, "then I must be home already," and walked away.

Outside, Katelizabeth met a couple of rogues and they wanted to go stealing. So Katelizabeth went to them and said, "I'll help you steal." The rascals thought she might know her way around the place and agreed. Katelizabeth went from house to house, crying, "Hey, everybody, what have you got for us to steal?" Thought the rascals, "This is going to be something," and wanted to get rid of Katelizabeth, so they said, "The pastor is growing turnips in a field outside the village, go pick us turnips." Katelizabeth went into the fields and began to pick but was so lazy she never straightened up, and a man who was passing saw her, stopped, and thought it was the devil rutting among the turnips, and ran to the pastor in the village and said, "Pastor, the devil's in your turnip field picking turnips." "Heavens!" answered the pastor, "and me with my lame foot; can't even get out there to exorcise him." Said the man, "I'll give you a piggyback," and carried him piggyback, and when they got out to the field Katelizabeth straightened up and stretched herself. "It's the devil!" cried the pastor and both ran away and the pastor in his great terror ran faster with his lame leg than the man who had carried him piggyback could run on his two healthy ones.

The Golden Bird

Once upon a time, in the old days, there was a king who had a beautiful garden behind his palace. In it there was a tree that bore golden apples. As the apples were getting ripe they were counted, but the very next morning one of them was missing. The king's sons told him about it, and he ordered that they should keep watch under the tree all night.

The king had three sons, the eldest of whom he sent into the garden as soon as it was night; but when midnight came he couldn't keep from going to sleep, and next morning another apple was missing. The next night the second son had to watch, but he had no better success; when midnight struck he fell asleep, and in the morning an apple was missing. Now it was the third son's time to watch, and he was all ready to, but the king didn't put much trust in him, and thought he'd be even less use than his brothers had been; at last, though, he let him go. The youth also lay down under the tree, watched, and didn't let himself go to sleep. As twelve struck, something rustled through the air, and in the moonlight he saw a bird flying along whose feathers were all shining with gold. The bird lit on the tree and had just pecked off an apple, when the youth shot an arrow at him. The bird flew away, but the arrow had struck his plumage, and one of his golden feathers fell down. The youth picked it up and next morning brought it to the king, and told him what had happened during the night. The king summoned his counselors, and every one of them declared that a feather like this was worth more than his whole kingdom put together. "If the feather is so precious," said the king, "just this one isn't enough for me. I must and will have the whole bird."

The oldest son set out, trusting to his own cleverness, and thought he'd as good as found the golden bird. When he'd gone some distance he saw a fox sitting on the edge of a wood, cocked his gun, and aimed at him. The fox said: "Don't shoot me, and in return I'll give you a piece of good advice. You're on the way to the golden bird, and this evening you'll come to a village where there're two inns right across from each other. One is all brightly lighted, and they're having a fine time inside. Don't go in, though, but go in the other, even if it looks bad."

"How can a foolish animal possibly give me reasonable advice?" thought the king's son, and pulled the trigger, but he missed the fox, who straightened out his tail and quickly ran off into the wood.

So then he set out on his way, and at evening came to the village where the two inns were. In one of them people were singing and dancing, the other had a wretched, dismal look. "I'd really be a fool," thought he, "if I went to that shabby inn and passed by the good one." So he went into the cheerful one, spent his time dancing and drinking, and forgot the bird, his father, and all good teachings.

When some time had gone by and the eldest son still hadn't come home, the second set out on his way to look for the golden bird. The fox met him just as he'd met the eldest, and gave him the same good advice that he paid no attention to. He came to the two inns; his brother was standing at the window of the one, from which the sound of merrymaking came, and called to him. He couldn't resist, went inside, and from then on lived only for pleasure.

Again some time went by, and then the king's youngest son wanted to set out and try his luck, but his father wouldn't allow it. "It's no use," said he. "He has even less chance than his brothers to find the golden bird, and if he meets with some misfortune he won't know what to do. He's not much, at best." But finally, since the youth gave him no peace, he let him go.

Again the fox was sitting on the edge of the wood, begged for his life, and gave his good advice. The youth was good-natured and said: "Don't worry, little fox. I won't hurt you."

"You won't regret it," answered the fox, "and to get along a little faster, climb onto my tail." And hardly had he sat down than the fox began to run, and away they went over hill and dale so that his hair whistled in the wind. When they came to the village, the youth got off, followed the good advice, and without even looking around went into the small inn, where he quietly spent the night. Next morning, as soon as he got out into the fields, there sat the fox already, and said: "I'll tell you what else you've got to do. Keep going straight ahead and finally you'll come to a castle in front of which a whole troop of soldiers will be lying. But don't you worry about them because they'll be snoring away, fast asleep. Walk through them and go straight into the castle, and go through all the rooms. Last of all you'll come to a chamber in which there's a wooden cage hanging, and in it a golden bird. Beside it is an empty gold cage, just for show, but be sure that you don't take the bird out of the plain cage and put it in the grand one, or you'll be in a mighty bad fix." After these words the fox straightened out his tail again, and the king's son got on; then away they went over hill and dale so that his hair whistled in the wind.

When he got to the castle, he found everything just as the fox had said. The king's son went into the chamber in which the golden bird sat in the wooden cage, with the golden one beside it. Three golden apples were lying in the room, too. Then he thought that it would be ridiculous to leave the beautiful bird in such an ugly, ordinary cage; he opened the door, seized it, and put it in the golden one. But that very instant the bird gave a piercing cry. The soldiers woke, rushed in, and led him off to prison. The next morning he was brought before a court and, since he confessed everything, sentenced to death. But the king said that he would spare him his life on one condition, that he bring him the golden horse that could run swifter than the wind, and then he'd give him the golden bird besides.

The king's son set out on his way, but he sighed and felt very sad, for how was he to find the golden horse? Then all at once he saw sitting by the road his old friend, the fox. "You see what's happened because you didn't listen to me," said the fox. "Cheer up, though, I'll look out for you and tell you how to get to the golden horse. You must go straight ahead, and that way you'll come to a castle in which the horse is standing in a stable. The grooms will be lying in front of the stable, but they'll be snoring away fast asleep, and you can easily lead out the golden horse. But one thing you've got to watch out for: put the plain wood and leather saddle on him, not the golden one hanging by it, or you'll be in a mighty bad fix." Then the fox straightened out his tail, the king's son got on, and away they went over hill and dale so that the wind whistled in his hair.

Everything happened just as the fox said it would. He went into the stable where the golden horse was standing, but when he was about to put the plain saddle on the horse, he thought: "It will spoil the looks of such a beautiful animal if I don't put on the good saddle it's entitled to." But hardly had the golden saddle touched it than the horse began to whinny loudly. The grooms woke up, seized the youth, and threw him in prison. The next morning he was sentenced to death by the court, but the king promised to grant him his life and the golden horse besides, if he could bring back the beautiful princess from the golden castle.

With a heavy heart the youth set out on his way, but soon, to his joy, he met the faithful fox. "I should just leave you to your bad luck," said the fox, "but I'm sorry for you and will help you out of your difficulty one more time. This road leads straight to the golden castle. You'll get there this evening, and tonight when everything is still, then the beautiful princess will go to the bathhouse to bathe. And when she goes in, leap out at her and give her a kiss. Then she'll follow you, and you can take her away with you. Only don't let her say goodbye to her parents, or you'll be in a mighty bad fix." Then the fox straightened out his tail, the king's son got on, and away they went over hill and dale so that the wind whistled in his hair.

When he got to the golden castle, it was just as the fox had said. He waited until midnight; when everyone lay in deep sleep and the beautiful maiden went to the bathhouse, he sprang out and gave her a kiss. She said that she'd gladly go with him, but implored him, with tears in her eyes, to let her say goodbye to her parents. At first he resisted her prayers, but when she wept and

wept and threw herself at his feet, he at last gave in. But hardly had the maiden got to her father's bedside than the youth was seized and put in prison.

Next morning the king said to him: "Your life is forfeit, and you'll be pardoned only if you move the mountain that stands in front of my window, that I can't see over, and you must manage it within eight days. If you succeed you shall have my daughter as your reward." The king's son started to dig and shovel without stopping, but when after seven days he saw how little he had accomplished and how all his work was as good as nothing, he became completely wretched and gave up all hope. But on the evening of the seventh day the fox appeared and said: "You don't deserve my looking out for you, but just walk over there and go to sleep. I'll do the work for you."

The next morning, when he woke up and looked out the window, the mountain had disappeared. Full of joy, the youth hurried to the king and told him that his condition had been satisfied, and that the king, whether he wanted to or not, must keep his word and give him his daughter.

211

So they set out together, and it wasn't long before the faithful fox came up to them. "You've certainly got the best thing, but the golden horse goes along with the maiden from the golden castle, too."

"How shall I get it?" asked the youth.

"That I'll tell you," answered the fox. "First bring the beautiful maiden to the king who sent you to the golden castle. Then they'll be overjoyed, they'll gladly give you the golden horse, and will lead it out to you. Get on it right away, offer your hand to all of them as you tell them goodbye, seize the beautiful maiden, and when you've got hold of her, swing her up and gallop away; and nobody will be able to catch you, for your horse is swifter than the wind."

Everything was accomplished successfully, and the king's son carried off the beautiful princess on the golden horse. The fox didn't stay behind, but said to the youth: "Now I'll help you get the golden bird too. When you're near the castle where the bird is, let the maiden dismount, and I'll take charge of her. Then ride the golden horse into the courtyard of the castle. They'll be overjoyed to see it, and will bring you out the golden bird. As soon as you've got the cage in your hand, gallop back to us and take the maiden away with you again."

When the plan had succeeded and the king's son was about to ride home with his treasures, the fox said: "Now you must reward me for my help."

"What do you want for it?" asked the youth.

"When we get to that wood over there, shoot me dead and chop off my head and feet."

"That would be a fine way to show my gratitude," said the king's son. "I couldn't possibly do that for you."

Said the fox: "If you won't do it, then I must leave you. But before I go I'll give you a piece of good advice. Watch out for two things: don't buy any gallows flesh and don't sit on the edge of any well." With that he ran off into the wood.

The youth thought: "That's a queer beast with some crazy ideas. Who would ever buy gallows flesh? And never have I had the slightest desire to sit down on the edge of a well."

He rode on with the beautiful maiden, and his road carried him back through the village where his two brothers had stayed. There was a great uproar and commotion, and when he asked what was wrong, they said that two men were about to be hanged. When he got nearer he saw that it was his brothers, who had done all kinds of wicked things and had wasted everything they owned. He asked whether they couldn't be set free. "If you'll pay for them," answered the people, "but why waste your money on these wicked men and buy them off?" But he didn't even hesitate, paid for them, and when they'd been freed, all of them went on their way together.

They came to the wood where the fox had met them first, and it was cool and pleasant inside and the sun burning hot, so the two brothers said: "Let's rest awhile here on the edge of this well and have something to eat and drink." He agreed, and while they were talking he forgot himself and sat down on the edge of the well, not suspecting any harm. But the two brothers pushed him over backwards into the well, took the maiden, the horse, and the bird, and rode home to their father. "Here we've brought you not just the golden bird, we've carried off the golden horse and the girl from the golden castle besides." The people were overjoyed, but the horse didn't eat, the bird didn't sing, and the maiden sat and wept.

The youngest brother hadn't perished, though. By good luck the well was dry, and he fell on some soft moss without being hurt, but wasn't able to get out again. Even in this extremity the faithful fox didn't forsake him. He came and jumped down to him, and scolded him for having forgotten his advice. "Still, though, I can't help it," said he. "I'll bring you back to the light of day." He told him to grasp his tail and hold on tight, and then he pulled him up.

"You're still not out of danger," said the fox. "Your brothers weren't sure you were dead, and have put guards around the forest who'll kill you if you let them see you." There by the road sat a poor man, and the youth changed clothes with him and in this way got to the king's palace. Nobody recognized him, but the bird began to sing, the horse began to eat, and the maiden stopped weeping. Astonished, the king asked: "What does this mean?"

Then the maiden said: "I don't know, but I was so sad, and now I'm so happy. I feel as if my true bridegroom had come." She told him everything that had happened, though the other brothers had threatened to kill her if she betrayed anything. The king ordered all the people in his palace to be brought before him; so the youth, looking like a poor beggar in his rags, came too. The maiden, though, recognized him immediately and threw her arms around his neck. The wicked brothers were seized and put to death, while he was married to the beautiful maiden and made the king's heir.

But what became of the poor fox? A long time afterward the king's son once again was walking in the wood, when the fox met him and said: "Now you have everything you can wish for, but my misery goes on without an end, and yet you have it in your power to free me." And once more he begged him to shoot him and chop off his head and feet. So he did, and no sooner was it done than the fox turned into a man, and was none other than the brother of the beautiful princess, freed at last from the spell under which he had lain. And now there was nothing lacking to their happiness, so long as they all lived.

Bearskin

Once upon a time there was a young fellow who enlisted in the army, carried himself bravely, and was always out in front where it rained bullets. As long as there was a war on, everything went well, but when they made peace he was discharged and the captain said he could go where he pleased. His parents had died, and he had no place to call home, so he went to his brothers and asked them to take care of him until a new war started. But the brothers were hardhearted men and said, "What are we to do with you! You are no good to us. Go make your own way as best you can." The soldier had nothing except his gun, which he took on his shoulder, and so he went out into the world. He came to a great heath on which there was nothing except a circle of trees. He sat down sadly and mused about his fate. I have no money, he thought, I have learned no trade except how to make war, and now they have made peace and don't need me any more. I can see that I must starve to death. All of a sudden he heard a great rustling and rushing, and when he looked around, there stood a stranger in a green coat, a fine-looking man but with a nasty horse's hoof. "I know what troubles you," the man said. "You shall have such an abundance of the world's goods that however hard you try, you'll never use it up, but first I have to make sure that you are not afraid. I don't want to waste my money." "A soldier and fear, they don't go together!" he answered. "Put me to the test." "Very well, then," said the man, "look behind you." The soldier turned around and saw a big bear trotting toward him and growling. "Oho," cried the soldier, "I'm going to tickle your nose for you so you won't feel like growling any more," took aim, and shot the bear in the muzzle so that it fell in a heap and never stirred again. "I can see," said the stranger, "you don't lack courage, but there is one other condition you must fulfill." "So long as it does not threaten my eternal soul," answered the soldier, who knew very well who it was standing before him, "I'm ready for anything." "Judge for yourself," answered Greencoat. "For the next seven years, you may neither wash yourself nor comb your beard or hair nor cut your nails nor pray the Our Father. And I will give you a jacket and an overcoat which you must wear all the time. If you die within the seven years you're mine, if you stay alive you are free and rich for the rest of your days." The soldier thought of his great need and how often he had faced death in the past, and was ready to dare it again, and so he agreed. The devil took off his green jacket and gave it to the soldier and said, "When you wear this coat and reach into your pocket, you will always find your hand full of money." Then he skinned the pelt off the bear and said, "This shall be your overcoat and your bed, because you must sleep in it, nor may you lie down on any other bed. And because of this costume you shall be called Bearskin." With that the devil disappeared.

The soldier put the coat on, reached into the pocket, and found the devil as good as his word. Then he hung the bearskin around his shoulders and went out into the world, was in good spirits, and left nothing undone that was good for him and bad for his money. In the first year things were still bearable. By the second year he began to look like a monster. His hair almost covered his face, his beard looked like a piece of coarse cloth, his fingers had grown claws, and his face was so dirty, if you had sowed cress on it, it would have sprouted. People ran away when they saw him, but he always gave money to the poor so they would pray for him not to die within the seven years. Because he paid well he always found a roof for his head wherever he went.

Now in the fourth year he came to an inn and the innkeeper refused to take him and would not even give him a place in the stable because he was afraid he might frighten the horses, but when Bearskin reached into his pocket and brought out a handful of ducats the innkeeper's heart softened. He let him have a room in the back, but he had to promise not to let anybody see him so as not to give the house a bad name.

In the evening Bearskin was sitting alone, wishing with all his heart that the seven years were past, when he heard loud wailing in the next room. He had a kind heart and opened the door and saw an old man crying with all his might, beating his hands together over his head. Bearskin came closer. The man jumped up and would have fled, but when he heard a human voice he let himself be calmed. Bearskin urged him so kindly, he even got him to disclose the cause of his misery. His fortune had dwindled a little at a time until he and his daughters were starving, and so poor was he that he could not even pay the innkeeper, who threatened to put him in jail. "If that's all that troubles you," said Bearskin, "I have plenty of money." He called the innkeeper, paid him off, and even put a purse of gold into the wretched man's pocket.

When the old man saw himself relieved of his worries he did not know how to show his gratitude. "Come with me," said he. "My daughters are marvels of beauty, choose one of them for your wife. When she hears what you have done for me, she will not refuse. You do look a little strange but she'll soon put you to rights." Bearskin liked the idea very well and went with him. When the oldest daughter caught sight of his face, it gave her such a fright she ran away screaming. The second one stayed and looked him over from head to foot but she said, "How can I take a husband who doesn't look human? I prefer the shaved bear who was on show here once, and pretended to be a man. At least he wore a fur coat like a hussar and had white gloves. If this one were merely ugly, I could get used to it." But the youngest said, "Dear Father, he must be a good man, who helped you in your need. If, in return, you promised him a bride, your word must be kept." It was a pity that Bearskin's face was covered with dirt and hair or one might have seen how his heart leaped for joy. He took a ring from his finger, broke it in two, gave her one half and kept the other himself. In her half he wrote his name and in his half he wrote her name and asked her to keep her piece safe. Then he took his leave

222

and said, "I have to travel another three years. If I come back we will celebrate our wedding, but if I don't return, you are free, because that means I am dead. But pray God to keep me alive."

The poor bride dressed herself all in black, and whenever she thought about her bridegroom, tears came into her eyes. From her sisters she had nothing but mockery and gibes. "Take care," said the eldest, "when you give him your hand, he will slap it with his paw." "Look out," said the second, "bears love sweets, and if he likes you he will gobble you up." "You must do everything he wants," the oldest started in again, "or he'll begin to growl," and the second one added, "But the wedding will be fun. Bears are good dancers." The bride said nothing and would not let them change her heart. But Bearskin roamed through the world from one place to another, did good deeds wherever he could, and gave generously to the poor so they would pray for him. Finally, when the last day of the seven years had dawned, he went back onto the heath and sat down under the circle of trees. Soon there was a great rustling and rushing, and the devil stood before him and looked at him crossly, threw him his old jacket, and asked for his green one back. "Not so fast," answered Bearskin, "first you have to clean me up." Willy-nilly, the devil had to fetch water and wash Bearskin and comb his hair and cut his nails, and soon he looked like a brave warrior again and much handsomer than before.

When, happily, the devil had taken himself off, Bearskin felt gay at heart. He went into town, put on a splendid velvet coat, got into a carriage drawn by four white horses, and drove to the house of his bride. Nobody knew him. The father took him for a high-ranking officer, brought him into the room where his daughters were sitting, and made him sit between the two eldest; they poured him wine, helped him to the choicest morsels, and thought they had never seen such a handsome man. But the bride sat across from him in her black dress, did not raise her eyes, and never said a word. Finally, when he asked the father to give him one of his daughters for a wife, the two eldest jumped up and ran into their room to put on their most splendid gowns because each imagined she was the chosen one. When the stranger was alone with his bride, he took

out his half of the ring, dropped it into a beaker of wine, and handed it across the table to her. She accepted, and when she had drunk it and found the half ring at the bottom, her heart began to beat. She took out the other half, which she wore on a ribbon around her neck, held the two pieces together and they matched perfectly, and he said, "I am your promised bridegroom whom you saw as Bearskin, but by God's grace I have my human form and am clean again." He came to her, embraced her, and gave her a kiss. At that moment the two sisters returned all dressed up, and when they saw that the handsome man belonged to their youngest sister and heard that it was Bearskin, they ran out of the room full of rage and fury. One drowned herself in the well, the other hanged herself on a tree. In the evening someone knocked at the door, and when the bridegroom opened it, it was the devil in his green coat, who said, "You see, now I've got two souls, instead of your one."

Godfather Death

A poor man had twelve children and worked night and day just to get enough bread for them to eat. Now when the thirteenth came into the world, he did not know what to do and in his misery ran out onto the great highway to ask the first person he met to be godfather. The first to come along was God, and he already knew what it was that weighed on the man's mind and said, "Poor man, I pity you. I will hold your child at the font and I will look after it and make it happy upon earth." "Who are you?" asked the man. "I am God."

"Then I don't want you for a godfather," the man said. "You give to the rich and let the poor go hungry." That was how the man talked because he did not understand how wisely God shares out wealth and poverty, and thus he turned from the Lord and walked on. Next came the Devil and said, "What is it you want? If you let me be godfather to your child, I will give him gold as much as he can use, and all the pleasures of the world besides." "Who are you?" asked the man. "I am the Devil." "Then I don't want you for a godfather," said the man. "You deceive and mislead mankind." He walked on and along came spindle-legged Death striding toward him and said, "Take me as godfather." The man asked, "Who are you?" "I am Death who makes all men equal." Said the man, "Then you're the one for me; you take rich and poor without distinction. You shall be godfather." Answered Death, "I will make your child rich and famous, because the one who has me for a friend shall want for nothing." The man said, "Next Sunday is the baptism. Be there in good time." Death appeared as he had promised and made a perfectly fine godfather.

When the boy was of age, the godfather walked in one

day, told him to come along, and led him out into the woods. He showed him an herb which grew there and said, "This is your christening gift. I shall make you into a famous doctor. When you are called to a patient's bedside I will appear and if I stand at the sick man's head you can boldly say that you will cure him and if you give him some of this herb he will recover. But if I stand at the sick man's feet, then he is mine, and you must say there is no help for him and no doctor on this earth could save him. But take care not to use the herb against my will or it could be the worse for you."

It wasn't long before the young man had become the most famous doctor in the whole world. "He looks at a patient and right away he knows how things stand, whether he will get better or if he's going to die." That is what they said about him, and from near and far the people came, took him to see the sick, and gave him so much money he became a rich man. Now it happened that the king fell ill. The doctor was summoned to say if he was going to get well. When he came to the bed, there stood Death at the feet of the sick man, so that no herb on earth could have done him any good. If I could only just this once outwit Death! thought the doctor. He'll be annoyed, I know, but I am his godchild and he's sure to turn a blind eye. I'll take my chance. And so he lifted the sick man and laid him the other way around so that Death was standing at his head. Then he gave him some of the herb and the king began to feel better and was soon in perfect health. But Death came toward the doctor, his face dark and angry, threatened him with raised forefinger, and said, "You have tricked me. This time I will let it pass because you are my godchild, but if you ever dare do such a thing again, you put your own head in the noose and it is you I shall carry away with me."

Soon after that, the king's daughter lapsed into a deep illness. She was his only child, he wept day and night until his eyes failed him and he let it be known that whoever saved the princess from death should become her husband and inherit the crown. When the doctor came to the sick girl's bed, he saw Death at her feet. He ought to have remembered his godfather's warning, but the great beauty of the princess and the happiness of becoming her husband so bedazzled him that he threw caution to the winds, nor did he see Death's angry glances and how he lifted his hand in the air and threatened him with his bony fist. He picked the sick girl up and laid her head where her feet had lain, then he gave her some of the herb and at once her cheeks reddened and life stirred anew.

When Death saw himself cheated of his property the second time, he strode toward the doctor on his long legs and said, "It is all up with you, and now it is your turn," grasped him harshly with his ice-cold hand so that the doctor could not resist, and led him to an underground cave, and here he saw thousands upon thousands of lights burning in rows without end, some big, some middle-sized, others small. Every moment some went out and others lit up so that the little flames seemed to be jumping here and there in perpetual exchange. "Look," said Death, "these are the life lights of mankind. The big ones belong to children, the middle-sized ones to married couples in their best years, the little ones belong to very old people. Yet children and the young often have only little lights." "Show me my life light," said the doctor, imagining that it must be one of

the big ones. Death pointed to a little stub threatening to go out and said, "Here it is." "Ah, dear godfather," said the terrified doctor, "light me a new one, do it, for my sake, so that I may enjoy my life and become king and marry the beautiful princess." "I cannot," answered Death. "A light must go out before a new one lights up." "Then set the old on top of a new one so it can go on burning when the first is finished," begged the doctor. Death made as if to grant his wish, reached for a tall new taper, but because he wanted revenge he purposely fumbled and the little stub fell over and went out. Thereupon the doctor sank to the ground and had himself fallen into the hands of death.

Many-Fur

Once upon a time there was a king and he had a wife who was the most beautiful woman in the world and had hair of pure gold and the two had a daughter as beautiful as her mother and her hair was just as golden. It happened that the queen became ill, and when she felt that she was about to die, she called the king and asked him to promise her that after she was dead he would marry no woman who was not as beautiful as she and had not the same golden hair, and when the king had promised, she died.

For a long time the king was so sad he never thought of a second wife, but finally his counselors urged him to remarry. And so messengers were sent to all the princesses but none was as beautiful as the queen who was dead and of course there was no one in the whole wide world who had such golden hair. One day the king's eye happened to fall on his daughter and he saw that she looked exactly like her mother and had the same golden hair and he thought, You'll never find anyone in all the world more beautiful than that, you have to marry your daughter, and at the same moment felt so great a love for her that he at once proclaimed his wishes to his counselors and to the princess. The counselors tried to talk him out of it, but in vain. The princess was horrified at her father's wicked plan but she was a clever girl and told the king that he must first get her three dresses, one as golden as the sun, one as white as the moon, and one that glittered like the stars; also a coat made of a thousand different kinds of fur, and every animal in the kingdom would have to give up a piece of its hide for it. But the king's desire was so fierce that he put his whole kingdom to work.

His huntsmen had to trap every animal and skin it and
the hides were made into a coat, and so it wasn't long
before he brought the princess what she had wished and
she said she would marry him the next day. But in the
night she gathered up the presents from her betrothed
—a gold ring, a little golden spinning wheel, and a little
golden reel—and put the three dresses of sun, moon,
and stars into a walnut shell; then she blackened her
face and hands with soot, put on her coat of many
furs, and ran away. All night she walked until she
came to a great forest where she would be safe, and
because she was tired she sat down in a hollow tree
and fell asleep.

It was already broad day and still she slept. It happened that the king to whom she was betrothed was
hunting nearby and his dogs came and ran around the
tree and sniffed at it. The king sent his huntsmen to
see what kind of animal might be hiding in the tree
and they came back and said it was the most peculiar
animal they had ever seen in all their lives. Its skin
was made of many furs and it was lying there fast
asleep. And so the king gave orders for the animal to

be caught and tied on the back of the wagon. But as the huntsmen were pulling it out they saw it was a girl and they tied her onto the back of the wagon and took her home with them. "Many-Fur," they said, "you'll do for the kitchen. You can carry wood and water and sweep up the ashes." And they gave her a little stall under the stair, where no daylight ever came: "Here's where you can live and sleep." And so now she had to work in the kitchen and helped the cook, plucked the chickens, raked the fire, cleaned the vegetables, and did all the dirty work. She worked so neatly, the cook was pleased with her and some evenings he called Many-Fur and gave her some of the leftovers to eat. But before the king went to bed she had to go upstairs to take off his boots and always when she had taken off one of them the king would throw it at her head.

In this way Many-Fur lived a long time, wretchedly enough. Ah, lovely princess, what is to become of you? Once there was a ball in the palace. Many-Fur thought, Here's a chance to get a glimpse of my dear sweetheart, and went to the cook and asked him if he wouldn't let her go upstairs for a while and stand at the door and look in on all the splendor. "Go along then," he said, "but don't stay away for more than half an hour, you still have all the ashes to sweep up tonight." And so Many-Fur took her oil lamp and went to her little stall, and washed the soot off her face and hands so that her beauty blossomed forth like a flower in the new spring; then she took off her coat of fur, opened the walnut, and took out the dress that shone like the sun. And when she was all dressed she went in and everybody made way for her because they thought it must be some elegant princess coming into the hall. The king at once took her hand for the dance and as they were dancing he thought, How this beautiful, strange princess resembles my dear bride, and the longer he looked at her the more she seemed to resemble her, so that he was almost sure. He was going to ask her when the dance was over, but as soon as she had finished she bowed and was gone before the king so much as knew what had happened. He sent to question the watchmen, but nobody had seen the princess leave the palace. Meanwhile, she had run to her little stall, quickly taken off her dress, blackened her face and hands, and put her coat of fur back on. Then she went into the kitchen and began sweeping the ashes, but the cook said, "Let that go till tomorrow. I want to go up too and watch the dancing for a bit, and you can cook the king's soup, but take care not to let a hair fall in the pot or I'll never give you anything to eat again." So Many-Fur cooked the king a bread soup and when it was done she put in the gold ring which he had given her. Now when the ball was over, the king asked for his bread soup and it tasted so good he thought he had never eaten a better one, and when he had finished and found the golden ring lying at the bottom, he looked at it closely and saw it was his wedding ring and he was astonished and could not understand how it had got there. He summoned the cook. The cook got angry with Many-Fur and said, "If you have let a hair fall in the soup, I'm going to beat you." But when the cook came upstairs, the king asked him who had cooked the soup because it was better than usual, and so he had to confess that Many-Fur had made it and the king told him to send her up.

When Many-Fur came before the king he said, "Who

are you and what are you doing in my palace? Where did you get the ring that was in my soup?" She answered, "I'm only a poor child who has lost her father and her mother. I have nothing and am good for nothing except to have boots thrown at my head, and I don't know anything about the ring either," and she ran away.

After that there was another ball and again Many-Fur asked the cook to let her go upstairs. The cook let her go but only for half an hour and then she was to come back and cook the king his bread soup. Many-Fur went to her little stall, washed herself clean, and took out the moon dress, more pure and shining than the new-fallen snow, and when she came upstairs the dance was just beginning and the king gave her his hand and danced with her and was no longer in any doubt that it was his bride because no one else, in all the world, had such golden hair; but when the dance was over the princess was gone and every effort was in vain, the king could not find her and had not been able to say one word to her. Meanwhile she had changed back into Many-Fur with her black face and hands and stood in the kitchen cooking the king's bread soup, and the cook had gone upstairs to watch the dancing. And when the soup was finished she put in the little golden spinning wheel. The king ate the soup and it seemed to him it tasted even better, and when he found the golden spinning wheel at the bottom he was even more astonished because it was the one he had given to his bride. The cook was sent for, and then Many-Fur, but again she would say only that she knew nothing and was only good to have boots thrown at her head.

And for the third time the king held a ball and hoped his bride would come again and was sure he could hold on to her. And again Many-Fur asked the cook if he wouldn't let her go upstairs. He scolded her and said, "You are a witch and put something in the soup; you can cook better than I." But she begged so hard and promised to do everything right, so he let her go upstairs for half an hour, and she put on the dress that glittered like the stars at night and went upstairs and danced with the king. It seemed to him that he

243

had never seen her as beautiful as this. While they were dancing he slipped a ring on her finger and he had ordered the dance to last a long, long time. But still he could not hold her or say a word to her, for when the dance was over she disappeared into the crowd before he had time to turn around. She got to her little stall and because it had been more than half an hour she quickly undressed, but in her hurry she could not blacken herself all over and left one finger white, and when she came to the kitchen the cook was already gone and so she quickly cooked the bread soup and put in the golden reel. The king found it as he had the ring and the spinning wheel and now he was sure that his bride was near because only she alone could have had these presents. Many-Fur was summoned and again she meant to talk her way out of it and make off, but as she was running away, the king saw the white finger and caught hold of her hand and he found the ring he had slipped onto it and tore off her coat and the golden hair came flowing out and it was his dearest bride and the cook was richly rewarded and they celebrated their wedding and lived happily until they died.

Rapunzel

Once upon a time there was a man and wife who had long wished for a child. Finally the woman was filled with hope and expected God would grant her wish. The couple had a little window in back of their house and you could look down into a magnificent garden full of the loveliest flowers and herbs. But the garden was surrounded by a high wall and nobody dared go in because it belonged to a great and powerful witch who was feared by all the world. One day the woman was standing by the window looking into the garden and saw a bed planted with the most beautiful lettuce, of the kind they call Rapunzel. It looked so fresh and green that she began to crave it and longed fiercely to taste the lettuce. Each day her longing grew and because she knew she could not have it, she began to pine and look pale and miserable. Her husband got frightened and said, "Dear wife, are you ill?" "Ah," said she, "if I cannot have some lettuce from the garden behind our house, I will die." The husband loved her very much, and said to himself, You can't let your wife die; fetch her some lettuce, whatever the cost may be. In the evening, therefore, at twilight, he clambered over the wall into the witch's garden, hurriedly dug up a handful of lettuce, and brought it home to his wife, and she made herself a salad right away and ate it ravenously. It tasted good, oh so good that the next day she craved it three times as much. If she was to have any peace, her husband must climb into the garden once again. And so at twilight he went back, but when he got down the other side of the wall he stood horrified, for there, standing right in front of him, was the witch. "How dare you come climbing into my garden, stealing my lettuce like a thief?" said she, and her eyes were angry. "You shall pay for this!" "Ah, no, please," cried the man. "Let justice be tempered with mercy! Only my despair made me do what I did. My wife saw your lettuce out of our window and felt such a craving that she had to have some, or die." And so the witch's anger began to cool and she said, "If that is so, I will allow you to take as much lettuce as you want on one condition: You must give me the child your wife brings into the world. It shall be well cared for. I will look after it like a mother." In his terror the man agreed to everything and no sooner had the wife been brought to bed than the witch appeared. She named the child Rapunzel and took it away with her.

Rapunzel grew into the most beautiful child under the sun. When she was twelve years old, the witch locked her up in a tower that stood in the forest and had neither stair nor door, only way at the top there was a little window. If the witch wanted to get inside, she came and stood at the bottom and called:

"Rapunzel, Rapunzel,
Let down your hair."

Rapunzel had magnificent long hair, fine as spun gold. Now when she heard the voice of the witch, she unfastened her braids, wound them around a hook on the window, and let the hair fall twenty feet to the ground below, and the witch climbed up.

After some years it happened that the king's son rode through the forest, past the tower, and heard singing so lovely he stood still and listened. It was Rapunzel in her loneliness, who made the time pass by letting her sweet voice ring through the forest. The prince wanted to climb up the tower and looked for the door but could not find one. So he rode home, but the singing had so moved his heart he came back to the forest day after day and listened. Once, when he was standing there behind a tree, he saw how a witch came along and heard her calling:

"Rapunzel, Rapunzel,
Let down your hair."

And then Rapunzel let her braids down and the witch climbed up. "If that's the ladder one takes to the top, I'll try my luck too." Next day, when it began to get dark, he went to the tower and called:

"Rapunzel, Rapunzel,
Let down your hair."

And the hair was let down and the prince climbed up.

At first Rapunzel was very much frightened when a man stepped in, because her eyes had never seen anything like him before, but the prince spoke very kindly to her and told her how his heart had been so moved by her singing he had wanted to see her. And so Rapunzel lost her fear, and when he asked her if she would take him for her husband and she saw how young and beautiful he was, she thought, He will love me better than my old godmother, and said, "Yes," and put her hand in his hand. She said, "I would like to go with you but I don't know how to get down from here. Every time you come, bring a skein of silk with you. I will braid a ladder and when the ladder is finished I will climb down and you will take me on your horse." Until that time

251

the prince was to come to her every evening, for by day came the old woman. The witch knew nothing about all this until one day Rapunzel opened her mouth and said, "Tell me, Godmother, why is it you are so much harder to pull up than the young prince? He's with me in the twinkling of an eye." "Oh, wicked child!" cried the witch. "What is this! I thought I had kept you from all the world and still you deceive me," and in her fury she grasped Rapunzel's lovely hair, wound it a number of times around her left hand, and with her right hand seized a pair of scissors and snip snap, the beautiful braids lay on the floor. And so pitiless was she that she took poor Rapunzel into a wilderness and left her there to live in great misery and need.

On the evening of the day on which she had banished Rapunzel, the witch tied the severed braids to the hook at the window, and when the prince came and called:

"Rapunzel, Rapunzel,
Let down your hair,"

she let the hair down. The prince climbed up and found not his dearest Rapunzel but the witch looking at him

with her wicked, venomous eyes. "Ah, ha," cried she mockingly, "you come to fetch your ladylove, but the pretty bird has flown the nest and stopped singing. The cat's got it and will scratch out your eyes too. You have lost Rapunzel and will never see her again." The prince was beside himself with grief and in his despair jumped out of the tower. His life was saved but he had fallen into thorns that pierced his eyes. And so he stumbled blindly about the forest, living on roots and berries, and did nothing but wail and weep for the loss of his dearest wife. And so for years he wandered in misery; finally he came into the wilderness where Rapunzel lived meagerly with her twin children, a boy and a girl, whom she had brought into the world. He heard her voice and it sounded so familiar to him. He walked toward it and Rapunzel recognized him and fell around his neck and cried. Two of her tears moistened his eyes and they regained their light and he could see as well as ever. He took her to his kingdom, where he was received with joy, and they lived happily and cheerfully for many years to come.

Snow-White and the Seven Dwarfs

Once it was the middle of winter, and the snowflakes fell from the sky like feathers. At a window with a frame of ebony a queen sat and sewed. And as she sewed and looked out at the snow, she pricked her finger with the needle, and three drops of blood fell in the snow. And in the white snow the red looked so beautiful that she thought to herself: "If only I had a child as white as snow, as red as blood, and as black as the wood in the window frame!" And after a while she had a little daughter as white as snow, as red as blood, and with hair as black as ebony, and because of that she was called Snow-White. And when the child was born, the queen died.

After a year the king took himself another wife. She was a beautiful woman, but she was proud and haughty and could not bear that anyone should be more beautiful than she. She had a wonderful mirror, and when she stood in front of it and looked in it and said:

> "Mirror, mirror on the wall,
> Who is fairest of us all?"

then the mirror would answer:

> "Queen, thou art the fairest of us all!"

Then she was satisfied, because she knew that the mirror spoke the truth.

But Snow-White kept growing, and kept growing more beautiful, and when she was seven years old, she was as beautiful as the bright day, and more beautiful than the Queen herself. Once when she asked her mirror:

> "Mirror, mirror on the wall,
> Who is fairest of us all?"

it answered:

> "Queen, thou art the fairest in this hall,
> But Snow-White's fairer than us all."

Then the Queen was horrified, and grew yellow and green with envy. From that hour on, whenever she saw Snow-White the heart in her body would turn over, she hated the girl so. And envy and pride, like weeds, kept growing higher and higher in her heart, so that day and night she had no peace. Then she called a huntsman and said: "Take the child out into the forest, I don't want to lay eyes on her again. You kill her, and bring me her lung and liver as a token."

The hunter obeyed, and took her out, and when he had drawn his hunting knife and was about to pierce Snow-White's innocent heart, she began to weep and said: "Oh, dear huntsman, spare my life! I'll run off into the wild forest and never come home again." And because she was so beautiful, the huntsman pitied her and said: "Run away then, you poor child."

"Soon the wild beasts will have eaten you," he thought, and yet it was as if a stone had been lifted from his heart not to have to kill her. And as a young boar just then came running by, he killed it, cut out its lung and liver, and brought them to the Queen as a token. The cook had to cook them in salt, and the wicked woman ate them up and thought that she had eaten Snow-White's lung and liver.

Now the poor child was all, all alone in the great forest, and so terrified that she stared at all the leaves on the trees and didn't know what to do. She began to run, and ran over the sharp stones and through the thorns, and the wild beasts sprang past her, but they did her no harm. She ran on till her feet wouldn't go any farther, and when it was almost evening she saw a little house and went inside to rest. Inside the house everything was small, but cleaner and neater than words will say. In the middle there stood a little table with a white tablecloth, and on it were seven little plates, each plate with its own spoon, and besides that, seven little knives and forks and seven little mugs. Against the wall were seven little beds, all in a row, spread with snow-white sheets. Because she was so hungry and thirsty, Snow-White ate a little of the vegetables and bread from each of the little plates, and drank a drop of wine from each little mug, since she didn't want to take all of anybody's. After that, because she was so tired, she lay down in a bed, but not a one would fit; this one was too long, the other was too short, and so on, until finally the seventh was just right, and she lay down in it, said her prayers, and went to sleep.

As soon as it had got all dark, the owners of the house came back. These were seven dwarfs who dug and delved for ore in the mountains. They lighted their seven little candles, and as soon as it got light in their little house, they saw that someone had been inside, because everything wasn't the way they'd left it.

The first said: "Who's been sitting in my little chair?"

The second said: "Who's been eating out of my little plate?"

The third said: "Who's been taking some of my bread?"

The fourth said: "Who's been eating my vegetables?"

The fifth said: "Who's been using my little fork?"

The sixth said: "Who's been cutting with my little knife?"

The seventh said: "Who's been drinking out of my little mug?"

Then the first looked around and saw that his bed was a little mussed, so he said: "Who's been lying on my little bed?" The others came running and cried out: "Someone's been lying in mine too." But the seventh, when he looked in his bed, saw Snow-White, who was lying in it fast asleep.

He called the others, who came running up and shouted in astonishment, holding up their little candles so that the light shone on Snow-White. "Oh my goodness gracious! Oh my goodness gracious!" cried they, "how beautiful the child is!" And they were so happy that they didn't wake her, but let her go on sleeping in the little bed. The seventh dwarf, though, slept with the others, an hour with each, till the night was over.

When it was morning Snow-White awoke, and when she saw the seven dwarfs she was frightened. They were friendly, though, and asked: "What's your name?"

"I'm named Snow-White," she answered.

"How did you get to our house?" went on the dwarfs. Then she told them that her stepmother had tried to have her killed, but that the huntsman had spared her life, and that she'd run the whole day and at last had found their house.

The dwarfs said: "If you'll look after our house for us, cook, make the beds, wash, sew, and knit, and if you'll keep everything clean and neat, then you can stay with us, and you shall lack for nothing."

"Yes," said Snow-White, "with all my heart," and stayed with them. She kept their house in order: in the morning the dwarfs went to the mountains and looked for gold and ores, in the evening they came back, and then their food had to be ready for them. In the daytime the little girl was alone, so the good dwarfs warned her and said: "Watch out for your stepmother. Soon she'll know you're here; be sure not to let anybody inside."

But the Queen, since she thought she had eaten Snow-White's lung and liver, was sure that she was the fairest of all. But one day she stood before her mirror and said:

"Mirror, mirror on the wall,
Who is fairest of us all?"

Then the mirror answered:

"Queen, thou art the fairest that I see,
But over the hills, where the seven dwarfs dwell,
Snow-White is still alive and well,
And there is none so fair as she."

This horrified her, because she knew that the mirror never told a lie; and she saw that the hunter had betrayed her, and that Snow-White was still alive. And she thought and thought about how to kill her, for as long as she wasn't the fairest in all the land, her envy gave her no rest. And when at last she thought of something, she painted her face and dressed herself like an old peddler woman, and nobody could have recognized her. In this disguise she went over the seven mountains to the seven dwarfs' house, knocked at the door, and called: "Lovely things for sale! Lovely things for sale!"

Snow-White looked out of the window and called: "Good day, dear lady, what have you to sell?"

"Good things, lovely things," she answered, "bodice laces of all colors," and she pulled out one that was woven of many-colored silk.

"It will be all right to let in the good old woman," thought Snow-White, unbolted the door, and bought herself some pretty laces.

"Child," said the old woman, "how it does become you! Come, I'll lace you up properly." Snow-White hadn't the least suspicion, and let the old woman lace her up with the new laces. But she laced so tight and laced so fast that it took Snow-White's breath away, and she fell down as if she were dead. "Now you're the most beautiful again," said the Queen to herself, and hurried away.

Not long after, at evening, the seven dwarfs came home, but how shocked they were to see their dear Snow-White lying on the ground; and she didn't move and she didn't stir, as if she were dead. They lifted her up, and when they saw how tightly she was laced, they cut the laces in two; then she began to breathe a little, and little by little returned to consciousness. When the dwarfs heard what had happened, they said: "The old peddler woman was no one else but that wicked Queen; be careful, don't ever let another soul inside when we're not with you."

But the wicked Queen, as soon as she'd got home, stood in front of the mirror and asked:

> "Mirror, mirror on the wall,
> Who is fairest of us all?"

It answered the same as ever:

> "Queen, thou art the fairest that I see,
> But over the hills, where the seven dwarfs dwell,
> Snow-White is still alive and well,
> And there is none so fair as she."

When she heard this all the blood rushed to her heart, she was so horrified, for she saw plainly that Snow-White was alive again. "But now," said she, "I'll think of something that really will put an end to you," and with the help of witchcraft, which she understood, she made a poisoned comb. Then she dressed herself up and took the shape of another old woman. So she went over the seven mountains to the seven dwarfs' house, knocked on the door, and called: "Lovely things for sale! Lovely things for sale!"

Snow-White looked out and said: "You may as well

go on, I'm not allowed to let anybody in."

"But surely you're allowed to look," said the old woman, and she took out the poisoned comb and held it up. It looked so nice to the child that she let herself be fooled, and opened the door. When they'd agreed on the price the old woman said: "Now, for once, I'll comb your hair properly." Poor Snow-White didn't suspect anything, and let the old woman do as she pleased. But hardly had she put the comb in Snow-White's hair than the poison in it began to work, and the girl fell down unconscious. "You paragon of beauty," cried the wicked woman, "now you're done for," and went away.

By good luck, though, it was almost evening, when the seven dwarfs came home. When they saw Snow-White lying on the ground as if she were dead, right away they suspected the stepmother and looked and found the poisoned comb. Hardly had they drawn it out than Snow-White returned to consciousness, and told them what had happened. Then they warned her all over again to stay in the house and open the door to no one.

At home the Queen stood in front of the mirror and said:

"Mirror, mirror on the wall,
Who is fairest of us all?"

It answered the same as ever:

"Queen, thou art the fairest that I see,
But over the hills, where the seven dwarfs dwell,
Snow-White is still alive and well,
And there is none so fair as she."

When she heard the mirror say that, she shook with rage. "Snow-White shall die," cried she, "even if it costs me my own life!" Then she went to a very secret, lonely room that no one ever came to, and there she made a poisoned apple. On the outside it was beautiful, white with red cheeks, so that anyone who saw it wanted it; but whoever ate even the least bite of it would die. When the apple was ready she painted her face and disguised herself as a farmer's wife, and then went over the seven mountains to the seven dwarfs' house. She knocked, and Snow-White put her head out of the window and said: "I'm not allowed to let anybody in, the seven dwarfs told me not to."

"That's all right with me," answered the farmer's wife. "I'll get rid of my apples without any trouble. Here, I'll give you one."

"No," said Snow-White, "I'm afraid to take it."

"Are you afraid of poison?" said the old woman. "Look, I'll cut the apple in two halves; you eat the red cheek and I'll eat the white." But the apple was so cunningly made that only the red part was poisoned. Snow-White longed for the lovely apple, and when she saw that the old woman was eating it, she couldn't resist it any longer, put out her hand, and took the poisoned half. But hardly had she a bite of it in her mouth than she fell down on the ground dead. Then the Queen gave her a dreadful look, laughed aloud, and cried: "White as snow, red as blood, black as ebony! This time the dwarfs can't wake you!"

And when, at home, she asked the mirror:

"Mirror, mirror on the wall,
Who is fairest of us all?"

at last it answered:

"Queen, thou art the fairest of us all."

Then her envious heart had rest, as far as an envious heart can have rest.

When they came home at evening, the dwarfs found Snow-White lying on the ground. No breath came from her mouth, and she was dead. They lifted her up, looked to see if they could find anything poisonous, unlaced her, combed her hair, washed her with water and wine, but nothing helped; the dear child was dead and stayed dead. They laid her on a bier, and all seven of them sat down and wept for her, and wept for three whole days. Then they were going to bury her, but she still looked as fresh as though she were alive, and still had her beautiful red cheeks. They said: "We can't bury her in the black ground," and had made for her a coffin all of glass, into which one could see from every side, laid her in it, and wrote her name on it in golden letters, and that she was a king's daughter. Then they set the coffin out on the mountainside, and one of them always stayed by it and guarded it. And the animals, too, came and wept over Snow-White—first an owl, then a raven, and last of all a dove.

Now Snow-White lay in the coffin for a long, long

time, and her body didn't decay. She looked as if she were sleeping, for she was still as white as snow, as red as blood, and her hair was as black as ebony. But a king's son happened to come into the forest and went to the dwarfs' house to spend the night. He saw the coffin on the mountain, and the beautiful Snow-White inside, and read what was written on it in golden letters. Then he said to the dwarfs: "Let me have the coffin. I'll give you anything that you want for it."

But the dwarfs answered: "We wouldn't give it up for all the gold in the world."

Then he said: "Give it to me then, for I can't live without seeing Snow-White. I'll honor and prize her as my own beloved." When he spoke so, the good dwarfs took pity on him and gave him the coffin.

Now the king's son had his servants carry it away on their shoulders. They happened to stumble over a bush, and with the shock the poisoned piece of apple that Snow-White had bitten off came out of her throat. And in a little while she opened her eyes, lifted the lid of the coffin, sat up, and was alive again. "Oh, heavens, where am I?" cried she.

The king's son, full of joy, said: "You're with me," and told her what had happened, and said: "I love you more than anything in all the world. Come with me to my father's palace; you shall be my wife." And Snow-White loved him and went with him, and her wedding was celebrated with great pomp and splendor.

But Snow-White's wicked stepmother was invited to the feast. When she had put on her beautiful clothes, she stepped in front of the mirror and said:

> "Mirror, mirror on the wall,
> Who is fairest of us all?"

The mirror answered:

> "Queen, thou art the fairest in this hall,
> But the young queen's fairer than us all."

Then the wicked woman cursed and was so terrified and miserable, so completely miserable, that she didn't know what to do. At first she didn't want to go to the wedding at all, but it gave her no peace; she had to go and see the young queen. And as she went in she recognized Snow-White and, what with rage and terror, she stood there and couldn't move. But they had already put iron slippers over a fire of coals, and they brought them in with tongs and set them before her. Then she had to put on the red-hot slippers and dance till she dropped down dead.

Rabbit's Bride

There was a woman and she had a daughter and they lived in a beautiful cabbage garden. In the wintertime there came a rabbit and ate all the cabbages, so the woman said to the daughter, "Go in the garden and chase the rabbit away." Says the girl to the rabbit, "Shoo shoo, rabbit, you're eating all our cabbage." Says the rabbit, "Come, girl, get up on my rabbit tail and come to my rabbit hut with me." But the girl doesn't want to. Next day the rabbit comes back and eats the cabbage, and the woman says to the daughter, "Go in the garden and chase the rabbit away." Says the girl to the rabbit, "Shoo shoo, rabbit, you're eating all our cabbage." Says the rabbit, "Come, girl, get up on my rabbit tail and come to my rabbit hut with me." The girl doesn't want to. On the third day the rabbit comes again and eats the cabbage, and the woman says to the daughter, "Go in the garden and chase the rabbit away." Says the girl, "Shoo shoo, rabbit, you're eating up our cabbage." Says the rabbit, "Come, girl, get up on my rabbit tail and come to my rabbit hut with me." The girl gets up on his rabbit tail and the rabbit carries her way away to his little hut and says, "Now cook me some green cabbage with millet and I'll go invite the wedding guests. And so the wedding guests assembled. (And who were the wedding guests? I can tell you that because I know all about it: All the rabbits were there, and the crow to act as parson to marry the bride and groom, and the fox was the sexton and the altar stood under the rainbow.) But the girl was sad, because she was lonely. Comes the rabbit and says, "Open the door, open the door, the wedding guests are ready for the party." The bride says nothing and cries. Rabbit goes away; rabbit comes back and says, "Open the door, open the door, the wedding guests are hungry." Again the bride says nothing and cries. Rabbit goes away. Rabbit comes back and says, "Open the door, open the door, the wedding guests are waiting." But the bride says nothing. Rabbit goes away but she makes a puppet out of straw and her clothes and gives it the wooden spoon to hold and sets it up in front of the kettle of millet and goes home to her mother. Rabbit comes back again and says, "Open the door, open the door," and opens the door and knocks the puppet on the head and the cap falls off.

And so rabbit sees that it is not his bride and goes away and is sad.

The Two Journeymen

Hill and valley never meet, but God's children do, sometimes even the good and the bad ones. And so it happened that a cobbler and a tailor who plied their trade from one town to the next met on the road. The tailor was a pretty little fellow, always jolly and in good spirits. He saw the cobbler walking toward him and could tell his trade by his knapsack, so he sang a song to tease him:

"Sew a stitch and pull a thread,

Paste it right and left with wax,
Hammer, hammer in the tacks."

The cobbler, who could not take a joke, made a face as
if he'd swallowed vinegar and seemed about to take the
little tailor by the scruff of the neck, but the little fellow began to laugh, offered him his bottle, and said, "I
didn't mean it. Have a drink and wash down your bile."
The shoemaker took a powerful swallow and the thun-
dercloud began to pass from his face. He handed the
bottle back to the tailor and said, "I've done it justice.
They're always talking about drinking too much but
never about the great thirst. Shall you and I go on our
way together?" "It's fine with me," answered the tailor,
"so long as you're heading for a big city where there's
plenty of work." "Just what I had in mind," answered
the cobbler. "There's no money to be made in the
backwoods; country people would rather go barefoot."
And so they went on together, setting one foot before
the other like the weasel in the snow.

Time they had aplenty, these two, but little bread
to break. When they came to a town they would make

the rounds, calling on the men of their trade for work or handouts; and because the tailor looked so cheerful and pleasant and had such nice red cheeks, people liked giving to him, and if he was lucky the master's daughter let him have a kiss in the doorway to take along. When tailor and cobbler met again the tailor always had more in his knapsack than the bad-tempered cobbler, who would make a sour face and say, "The greater the scoundrel, the better his luck," but the tailor laughed, sang a song, and shared whatever he got with his friend. If his pocket tinkled with a couple of extra pennies, he'd call for the table to be laid and strike it in his delight, so that the glasses danced. His motto was "Easy come, easy go."

When they had been on the road for a while, they came to a great forest through which lay the way to the royal capital. But there were two paths and one took seven days, but the other took only two. Neither of the two journeymen knew which path was the shorter, so they sat down under an oak tree and talked over how they were to provide for themselves and how many days' bread they should carry with them. The cobbler said,

The Two Journeymen

"One must think further than one travels. I will take bread for seven days." "Go on!" said the tailor, "haul seven days' bread on your back like a beast of burden so you can't even look about you! I trust in God and never worry. The money in my pocket is as good in summer as it is in winter, but bread dries out in hot weather and gets moldy besides; nor is my coat longer than I need to cover my ankles. Why shouldn't we hit upon the right path? Bread for two days, and that's that." And so each bought his bread and hoped for the best.

Inside the forest it was still as in a church. No wind stirred, no brook babbled, no bird sang. No ray of light could pass through the thickly leaved branches. The cobbler spoke never a word; the heavy bread pressed down on his back so that the sweat poured over his gloomy, ill-humored face. But the tailor was gay and skipped along, whistling on a leaf, singing his little song, and thought, "God in his heaven must be glad that I'm so happy!" And so it went for two days, but on the third day, when the forest would not come to an end and the tailor had finished all his bread, his heart did sink way down, but he never lost hope, trusted in God and his good luck. On the evening of the third day he lay down hungry under a tree and got up hungry next morning. And so it went on the fourth day, and when the cobbler took his seat on a fallen tree to partake of his meal, there was nothing for the tailor to do but look on. If he begged for a piece of bread, the other laughed and mocked him and said, "You were always so happy, for once you'll feel what it's like to be unhappy. It's the bird who sings too early in the morning that the hawk strikes down before the night." In short, he had no mercy. But on the fifth morning the poor tailor was unable to get up and could barely speak for weakness. His cheeks were white and his eyes were red and so the cobbler said, "I will give you a little piece of bread today, but in return I will cut your right eye out." The unhappy tailor, who longed to stay alive, had no choice. He wept one last time with his two eyes, and then held them up to the cobbler, who had a heart of stone and cut out the tailor's right eye with a sharp knife. The tailor remembered what his mother always used to say when she caught him nibbling in the larder: "Eat what you will, and suffer what you must." When he had eaten his bit of bread so dearly bought, he got to his feet, forgot his misfortune, and comforted himself with the thought that he could still see well enough out of his other eye. But on the sixth day there was the hunger all over again and it nearly ate his heart out, and in the evening he fell down by a tree, and on the seventh day he could not get up for weakness, and death had him by the throat. And so the cobbler said, "I will be merciful once again and give you bread; but you must pay for it; I will cut out your other eye as well." And so the tailor understood the heedlessness of his life, begged the good Lord's forgiveness, and said, "Do what you will, I will suffer what I must. Only remember, Our Lord does not pass judgment each moment of the day, yet there shall come an hour when you will be punished for the evil you do me. I have not deserved it of you. In good times I shared with you whatever I had. My trade commands that one stitch chase another. If I have no eyes left I cannot sew and must go begging. Only do not leave me lying alone here after I am blind, or I shall perish." But the cobbler, who had driven God out of his heart, took the knife and cut out the tailor's other eye too. Then he gave him a piece of bread, handed him a stick, and led the tailor along behind him.

As the sun was setting they came out of the forest, and in a field near the edge of the forest stood a gallows and here the cobbler led the blind tailor and left him lying and went on his way. Out of weariness, pain, and hunger, the wretched man fell asleep and slept all night. When day dawned he woke but did not know where he was. On the gallows hung two poor sinners and on the head of each sat a crow, and one of the dead men began to speak: "Brother, are you awake?" "Yes, I am awake," answered the second. "Then I will tell you something," the first went on. "The dew which dripped down from the gallows over us last night could give the man who washes with it his eyesight back again. If the blind knew, there's many a one might have his eyes back who doesn't believe it possible." When the tailor heard this, he took out his handkerchief, pressed it to the grass, and when it was moist with dew he washed the sockets of his eyes with it. Immediately what the hanged man said came true: a pair of whole, healthy eyes filled his sockets. And the tailor saw the sun rising behind the

mountains. Before him, on the great plain, lay the imperial city with its splendid gates, and the hundred towers with golden buttons and crosses on their pinnacles began to glow. He could distinguish every leaf on the trees, saw the birds fly by and the gnats dancing in the air. He took a sewing needle from his pocket and threaded it as easily as ever, and his heart leaped for joy. He threw himself upon his knees, thanked God for the grace he had shown him, and said his morning blessing, nor did he forget to pray for the poor sinners hanging from the gallows like clappers in a bell, with the wind knocking one against the other. Then he took his bundle on his back, soon forgot the heartache he had suffered, and went singing and whistling on his way.

The first thing to cross his path was a brown foal cavorting in the open field. He grasped it by the mane, so as to swing himself up and ride into town, but the foal begged for its freedom. "I'm too young," it said. "Even a lightweight tailor like you would break my back, so let me go till I've grown strong. The time may come when I can make it up to you." "Run along," said the tailor. "I see that you're a flibbertigibbet just like me," and he spanked it over the rump with his switch so that it kicked its hind legs for joy, leaped over hedge and ditch, and chased off into the fields.

But the little tailor had eaten nothing since yesterday. "The sun fills my eyes," he said, "but where's the bread to fill my mouth? The first thing I run across that's anywhere near edible will have to be it." Just then, a stork came striding very gravely by. "Halt," cried the tailor, and grabbed it by the leg. "I don't know if you are edible or not, but my hunger doesn't leave me much choice. I'm going to cut off your head and roast you." "Don't do it," said the stork. "I am a sacred bird; nobody harms me, for I am very useful to mankind. Let me live, and I may repay you for it sometime or another." "Off you go, then, Cousin Longlegs," said the tailor. The stork rose into the air, letting his long legs dangle, and, without hurrying himself, flew away.

"This will never do," said the tailor to himself. "My hunger is getting worse and worse, and my stomach emptier and emptier. The next thing that crosses my path is lost." At that moment he saw a pair of ducks swimming on a pond. "You're just in time," he said, caught hold of one of them, and was about to wring its neck when the mother duck, who was hidden in the rushes, began to screech, making a great to-do, and came swimming up with her beak wide open, imploring him to have pity on her beloved children. "Only imagine," said she, "how your mother would carry on if someone did this to you." "Oh, all right," said the good-natured tailor, "you can keep your children," and set the captive back in the water. When he turned he was standing before a hollow tree and saw wild bees flying in and out. "Here's the reward for my good deed already," said the tailor. "This honey will revive me." But the queen bee came out and threatened him, saying, "If you touch my people and destroy my nest, our stingers shall pierce your skin like ten thousand fiery needles; but leave us in peace and go on your way and in return we will do you a service some day."

The little tailor saw there was nothing to be done here either. "Three empty platters," said he, "and nothing on the fourth is a poor sort of dinner." And so with his belly starving he dragged himself into the city, where the noon bell was pealing and the food at the inn was cooked and ready for him, and he sat down to dinner. When he had eaten his fill, he said, "And now I want some work," and walked around town looking for a master and soon found himself a good place, and because he had learned his trade from the ground up, it wasn't long before everyone wanted his new coat made by the little tailor. His fame grew day by day. "There's no way to improve my skill," said he, "yet every day I do better." And in the end the king appointed him Court Tailor.

But as it goes in this world, his former companion, the cobbler, had that same day been made Court Cobbler and when he caught sight of the tailor and saw that he had his two whole eyes again, his conscience tormented him. "Before he takes his revenge on me, I'll dig his grave for him," he thought. But he who digs another's grave falls in himself. In the evening, when he had closed up shop and dusk was falling, he sneaked off to the king and said, "Your majesty, that tailor is an impudent fellow. He has the gall to boast that he could find the crown lost in the olden days." "I'd like that," said the king, and the next morning he summoned the tailor and ordered him to produce the crown or leave town forever. "Oho," thought the tailor, "only a scoundrel gives more than he has. If this cantankerous king asks me to do what no man can, I won't wait till morning, I'll leave right now." And so he packed his bundle, but when he got outside the city gate he was sorry to leave his good fortune and face with his backside the town which had done so well by him.

He came to the pond where he had made the acquaintance of the ducks, and the old one, whose young he had spared, happened to be sitting on the shore preening herself with her beak. She knew him at once and asked why he hung his head. "You'll understand when you hear what happened to me," answered the tailor and told her his fate. "If that's all it is," said the duck, "there's no problem. The crown fell in the water and is lying on the bottom. We'll have it up in no time. You spread your handkerchief on the shore." The duck dove down with her twelve young ones and was back in five minutes, sitting in the middle of the crown, which rested on her feathers, and the twelve ducklings swam all around her, their beaks underneath the crown to help carry it. You can't imagine how it glittered in the sun like a hundred thousand brilliants. The tailor tied together the four corners of the cloth and brought the crown to the king, who was overjoyed and hung a golden chain around the tailor's neck.

When the cobbler saw that one trick had misfired, he thought up a second, presented himself before the king, and said, "Your majesty, that tailor is becoming impudent again. He has the gall to boast he could make a wax model of the whole palace with everything in it, freestanding or fixed, inside and out." The king summoned the tailor and ordered him to make a wax model of the whole palace and everything in it, free-standing or fixed, inside and out, and if he couldn't do it or left out so much as a nail in the wall, he would sit out the rest of his life in an underground prison. The tailor thought, "Worse and worse. No man can put up with this," threw his bundle across his shoulders, and marched off. When he came to the hollow tree, he sat down and hung his head. The bees flew out and the queen asked him if he had a stiff neck, the way he held his head.

"Oh no," answered the tailor, "it's a very different kind of trouble that makes me so sad," and told them what the king demanded of him. The bees began to buzz and hum among themselves and the queen bee said, "You just go back home, but tomorrow about this time come back, bring a nice big cloth, and everything will be all right." And so he went home, but the bees flew straight to the royal palace and through the open window, crept around in all the corners, and inspected every last thing. Then they flew back and copied everything in wax at such speed you would have thought you saw the palace growing before your eyes. It was all done by evening, and next morning, when the tailor came, there stood the whole splendid edifice, and not a nail in the wall, not a tile in the roof was missing, and it was delicate and snow-white and smelled sweet as honey besides. The tailor wrapped it carefully in his cloth and brought it to the king, who could not get over his surprise, set it up in the grandest of the halls, and in return made the tailor a present of a big stone house.

But the cobbler did not give up, appeared before the king a third time, and said, "Your majesty, the tailor has heard that no water will spring in the palace grounds and has the gall to boast that he could make it rise in the middle of your courtyard, man-high and clear as crystal." And so the king had the tailor brought in and said, "If by tomorrow there's no fountain springing man-high in my courtyard, as you have promised, the executioner shall, in that very spot, make you shorter by a head." The poor tailor did not stay to consider, but hurried out of the city gate, and because this time it was a matter of his very life, the tears rolled down his cheeks.

As he was walking full of grief, the foal whom he had given its freedom, and who had turned into a handsome, full-grown horse, came galloping along. "The time has come," it said, "when I can repay your good deed. I know what troubles you, but help is at hand. Just get up on my back. I could carry two your size." The tailor took heart again, mounted his back in one leap, and the horse ran to town at full gallop, straight into the royal courtyard, circled three times quick as lightning, and the third time crashed to the ground. In that same instant came a thunderous roar, a piece of earth flew like a cannon ball out of the middle of the courtyard, way into the air, over the palace, and in its wake rose a jet of water high as man and horse and clear as crystal, and caught the rays of the sun that danced upon it. When the king saw it, he stood up in amazement and came and embraced the little tailor in sight of all the people.

But his luck did not last. The king had daughters aplenty, one more beautiful than the next, but not a single son. And so the spiteful cobbler betook himself to the king a fourth time and said, "Your majesty, the tailor will not give up his impudent boasting. Now he has the gall to say that if he wished, he could have a son delivered to your majesty, by air." The king summoned the tailor and said, "If you have a son brought to me within nine days, you shall marry my eldest daughter." "The reward is certainly great," thought the little tailor, "and one would go out of one's way for it, but these are cherries that hang out of my reach. If I climb after them, the bough will break and I'll fall all the way down." He went home and sat down cross-legged on his worktable to consider what was to be done. "It'll never work," he finally cried. "There's no living in peace here." He tied his bundle and hurried out of the city gate. When he came to the meadow he caught sight of his old friend the stork, walking like some sage, up and down, stopping once in a while to make a close study of a frog he was about to swallow. The stork came to greet him. "I see," he began, "that you have your knapsack on your back. Why do you want to leave the city?" The tailor told him of the king's demand which he could not fulfill and bemoaned his ill fortune. "Don't grow any gray hairs over it," answered the stork. "I will help you in your need. I've been bringing the little babies to this city for a long while and there's no reason why I shouldn't fetch a little baby prince out of the well for once. You go home, don't fret. Nine days from today come to the court and I will be there too." The tailor went home and was at the palace in good time. It wasn't long before the stork came flying and knocked at the window. The tailor opened it and Cousin Longlegs stepped in cautiously and walked with measured tread over the smooth marble floors. In his beak he had a child, beautiful as an angel, who stretched his hands toward the queen. The stork put the baby in her lap and she hugged it and kissed it and was beside herself with joy. Before he flew away, the stork took his traveling bag from his shoulder and gave it to the queen. Inside were little paper cones full of colored candies to be shared among the little princesses. Only the eldest didn't get any. She got the happy tailor for a husband. "I feel," said the tailor, "as if I'd won first prize. My mother was right after all. She always said if a man trusts in God, and if he's lucky, he cannot fail."

The cobbler had to make the shoes in which the little tailor danced at his wedding and afterwards he was ordered to leave the town forever. The way to the forest led him past the gallows. Worn out with fury, anger, and the day's heat, he threw himself down, and as he closed his eyes to sleep, the two crows sitting on the hanged men's heads plummeted down with a loud screech and hacked out his two eyes. The cobbler in his madness ran into the forest, where he must have perished. Nobody has seen him since or heard anything about him.

Ferdinand Faithful
and Ferdinand Unfaithful

Once upon a time there was a man and a woman. As long as they were rich they didn't have any children, but when they became poor they got a little boy. They couldn't find him a godfather, so the man said he'd run over to the next village and see if he couldn't get one there. And as he was walking along he met a poor man who asked him where he was going. He said he was looking for a godfather for his little boy, because he was so poor nobody wanted to be godfather. "Oh," said the poor man, "you are poor and I am poor so I'll be the godfather, but I'm too poor to give the child anything. Go and tell the midwife to bring the child to the church." When everyone gets to the church, there's the beggar already inside and he gives the child the name of Ferdinand faithful.

Now as they were coming out, the beggar said, "You go along home. I can't give you anything so don't you give me anything either." But to the midwife he gave a key and told her to go home and give it to the father to keep until the child was fourteen years old, and then the boy should go up to the heath and there would be a castle with a keyhole which the key would fit and whatever was inside belonged to him. Now one day, when the child was seven years old and had grown a good deal, he went out to play with the other boys, and each one had got more from his godfather than the next. He was the only one who had nothing to tell and he cried and went home and said to his father, "Didn't I get anything at all from my godfather?" "Oh, yes," said the father. "What you got was a key. If there's a castle with a keyhole standing up on the heath, you just go over and unlock it." And so he went up on the heath

299

but there was no castle to be heard or seen. Seven years later, when he is fourteen years old, he goes up again and there's the castle and he unlocks it and there's nothing in it except a horse, a white one, and the boy is so pleased with his horse he gets on its back and gallops home to his father. "Now I have a horse, I want to travel," says he.

Off he goes, and as he is riding along there's this writing quill lying on the road. First he is going to pick it up but then he thinks to himself, You could really let it lie where it is, you are sure to find a quill wherever you're going, if you happen to need one, and as he is riding away, he hears something calling behind him, "Ferdinand faithful, take it with you." He looks around, doesn't see anybody, goes back, and picks it up. When he has ridden for a while he comes to a river and there is a fish lying on the shore flapping and snapping for air, and so he says, "Wait a moment, my dear fish, and I'll help you get back into the water," takes it by the tail, and throws it into the river, and the fish sticks its head out of the water and says, "Because you helped me out of the mud, I'll give you a flute to pipe on. If you're ever in need, pipe, and I will come and help you, or if you should ever drop anything into the water, you just pipe and I will hand it up to you." And so he rides on and there comes this man walking along and asks him where he is going. "Oh, to the next place." And what's his name? "Ferdinand faithful." "Look at that, then we have almost the same name! I am called Ferdinand unfaithful." So they continue on their way together as far as the next village and go into the inn.

Now the trouble was that this Ferdinand unfaithful knew everything the other person was thinking or planning. He knew these things by means of all kinds of evil arts. Now in this inn there was a stouthearted girl with a nice open face who carried herself so nicely and she fell in love with Ferdinand faithful because he was a nice-looking boy and she asked him where he was going. Oh, traveling around. And so she said why didn't he stay here, there was a king in the country and he was sure to want a servant or an outrider and why not go into his service. He answered that he couldn't very well go to someone and offer himself, but the girl said, "Well, then I'll do it for you." And so she went right to the king and told him she knew a nice-looking servant for him. That was fine by the king and he had him summoned and would have made him his servant, but Ferdinand faithful liked being an outrider better because wherever his horse was, that's where he wanted to be, and so the king made him an outrider. When Ferdinand unfaithful found out about this he said to the girl, "Wait a minute, are you going to help him and not me?" "Oh," said the girl, "I'll help you too." She thought, You'd better stay friends with this one because you can't trust him, so she goes to the king and offers him as a servant and that's fine with the king.

Now mornings, when Ferdinand unfaithful was dressing his master, the king was always complaining and carrying on: "Oh, if I only had my beloved here with me." Ferdinand unfaithful was always looking to make trouble for Ferdinand faithful and one day, when the king was complaining again, he said, "You have your outrider. Why don't you send him to go and get her for you and if he doesn't, let his head be laid at his feet." And so the king has Ferdinand faithful summoned and tells him he has a beloved there and there and to go get her, and if he doesn't, he shall die.

Ferdinand faithful went to his white horse in the stable and cried and complained. "Oh, what an unhappy creature am I," but he hears somebody calling behind him: "Ferdinand faithful, what are you crying for?" He looks around, doesn't see anybody, and goes on lamenting and complaining: "Oh, my dear horse, I have to leave you now and I'm going to die." And again there is this voice calling, "Ferdinand faithful, what are you crying for?" and only now does he see that it is his little white horse that is asking the question. "Is that you, dear horse? And can you talk?" and he goes on, "I am supposed to go there and there to fetch the bride. You wouldn't know how I am to go about it, would you?" and so the white horse answers, "You just go to the king and tell him to give you what you need and you will go and fetch the bride. If he gives you a ship full of meat and a ship full of bread, you'll manage everything because there are great big giants on the water and if you didn't bring them any meat they would tear you apart, and there are great big birds who would pick the eyes out of your head if you didn't bring any bread for them." And so the king ordered all the butchers in the land to butcher and all the bakers to bake so as to fill the ships. And when they are filled up, the little white horse says to Ferdinand faithful, "Now get on my back and ride me onto the boat and when the giants come say:

> "Hush up, my little giants.
> I've not forgotten you
> And brought you something too.

and when the birds come, then you say again:

> "Hush up, dear little birdies.
> I've not forgotten you
> And brought you something too.

Then they won't do you any harm and when you get to the castle the giants will help you. Go into the castle and take a couple of giants with you and the princess will be lying there, asleep, but you mustn't wake her. Just have the giants pick her up, bed and all, and carry

her into the ship." And everything happened just as the horse had said and Ferdinand faithful gave the giants and the birds what he had brought for them and in return the giants helped carry the princess in her bed. But when she comes to the king she says she cannot live, she has to have her papers that were left behind in the castle. And so Ferdinand faithful, at the instigation of Ferdinand unfaithful, is summoned and the king orders him to go fetch the papers from the castle or die. And so he goes back to the stable and cries and says, "Dear horse, now I have to leave you again. Whatever are we going to do?" And so the white horse says he should load up the ships again. (And so it goes just like the last time and the giants and the birds are fed and appeased with the meat.) When they get to the castle the white horse says he should walk into the princess's bedroom, the papers are on the desk. And so Ferdinand faithful goes in and fetches them. And when they are on the high seas he drops his writing quill in the water and the horse says, "Now I can't help you," and he remembers the flute and starts piping and the fish comes and has the quill in his mouth and reaches it up to him. Then he brings the papers to the castle and the wedding is celebrated.

However, the queen did not like the king very much because he did not have a nose; she liked Ferdinand faithful. So one day, when all the gentlemen of the court were assembled, the queen said that she knew a good trick: she could chop off someone's head and put it back again and someone should come and try it. Nobody wanted to be first, and so Ferdinand faithful, again at the instigation of Ferdinand unfaithful, had to be the one, and she chopped off his head and put it back on again and it healed right away so that he looked as if he had a red thread around his neck. And so the king said, "My child, where did you learn that?" "Oh, well," said she, "it's a talent I have. Shall I try it on you?" "Oh, yes," says he, and she chops off his head but doesn't put it back and acts as if she can't get it on again. It just will not and will not stay put. And so the king is buried and she marries Ferdinand faithful.

But Ferdinand faithful is always riding his white horse. One day when he is sitting on its back, it tells him to ride to a new pasture, it'll let him know which one, and to gallop three times around it, and when he has done this the white horse stands up on its hind legs and turns into a prince.

Mrs. Gertrude

Once upon a time there was a little girl and she was obstinate and willful and did not obey her parents when they spoke to her. What good can come to such a child? One day she said to her parents, "I've heard so much talk about Mrs. Gertrude I want to go and see her. People say her house is very strange and they say there are such queer goings on there that I've become curious." Her parents strictly forbade her and said, "Mrs. Gertrude is an evil woman who does wicked things. If you go there, you are no longer our child." But the girl

paid no attention, and though her parents had told her no, went anyway, and when she got to Mrs. Gertrude, Mrs. Gertrude said, "Why are you so pale?" "Ah," the girl answered, trembling all over, "because I'm frightened at the things I've seen." "What have you seen?" "I saw a black man on your stairs." "That was a collier." "Then I saw a green man." "That was a hunter." "And then I saw a man red as blood." "That was a butcher." "Ah, but, Mrs. Gertrude, it made my skin crawl when I looked through the window and didn't see you but it must have been the devil himself with his head on fire." "Oho," said she, "so you have seen the witch in her true ornament. I have been expecting you a long time and have hankered for you, you're going to brighten up my house for me." And she changed the little girl into a log and threw it into the fire. And when it was at full glow she sat down beside it, warmed herself, and said, "There now, isn't that nice and bright!"

The Juniper Tree

It is a long time ago now, as much as two thousand years maybe, that there was a rich man and he had a wife and she was beautiful and good, and they loved each other very much but they had no children even though they wanted some so much, the wife prayed and prayed for one both day and night, and still they did not and they did not get one. In front of their house was a yard and in the yard stood a juniper tree. Once, in wintertime, the woman stood under the tree and peeled herself an apple, and as she was peeling the apple she cut her finger and the blood fell onto the snow. "Ah," said the woman and sighed a deep sigh, and she looked at the blood before her and her heart ached. "If I only had a child as red as blood and as white as snow." And as she said it, it made her feel very happy, as if it was really going to happen. And so she went into the house, and a month went by, the snow was gone; and two months, and everything was green; and three months, and the flowers came up out of the ground; and four months, and all the trees in the woods sprouted and the green branches grew dense and tangled with one another and the little birds sang so that the woods echoed, and the blossoms fell from the trees; and so five months were gone, and she stood under the juniper tree and it smelled so sweet her heart leaped and she fell on her knees and was beside herself with happiness; and when six months had gone by, the fruit grew round and heavy and she was very still; and seven months, and she snatched the juniper berries and ate them so greedily she became sad and ill; and so the eighth month went by, and she called her husband and cried and said, "When I die, bury me under the juniper." And she was comforted and felt happy, but when the nine months were gone, she had a child as white as snow and as red as blood and when she saw it she was so happy that she died.

And so her husband buried her under the juniper tree and began to cry and cried very bitterly; and then for a time he cried more gently and when he had cried some more he stopped crying and more time passed and he took himself another wife.

By the second wife he had a daughter, but the child of his first wife was a little son as red as blood and as white as snow. Now when the woman looked at her daughter she loved her so, but looking at the little boy cut her to the heart. It seemed that wherever he was standing, he was always in her way and then she kept wondering how to get the whole fortune just for her daughter, and the evil one got into her so that she began to hate the little boy and would push him around from one corner to the other and punch him here and pinch him there so that the poor child was always in a fright. When he came home from school there was no quiet place where he could be.

Once the woman had gone upstairs and her little daughter came up too and said, "Mother, can I have an apple?" "Yes, my child," said the woman and gave her a beautiful apple out of the chest. Now this chest had a great heavy lid with a sharp iron lock. "Mother," said the little daughter, "couldn't brother have one too?" This upset the woman but she said, "He can have one when he gets back from school." And as she looked out of the window she saw him coming and it was just as if the devil got into her and she reached out and snatched the apple out of her daughter's hand and said, "You can't have one till your brother comes," and threw the apple back into the chest and closed the lid. And then the little boy came in the door and the evil one made her speak kindly to him and she said, "My son, would you like an apple?" and looked at him full of hatred. "Mother," said the little boy, "how strange and wild you look! Please give me an apple." And it was as if she must still draw him on and she said, "Come with me," and lifted up the lid. "You can pick out your own apple." And as the little boy leaned in, the evil one spoke in her ear. Crunch! she slammed the lid shut so

317

that the head flew off and rolled among the red apples.
And now terror overwhelmed her and she thought,
"How can I get myself out of this?" and so she went up
to her room, to her wardrobe, and out of the top drawer
she took a white cloth and set the head back on the neck
and tied the scarf around it in such a way that you
couldn't see anything and set him on a chair in front of
the door and put the apple in his hand.

And little Ann Marie came into the kitchen where
her mother was standing by the fire with a pot of hot
water in front of her that she kept stirring around and
around. "Mother," said Ann Marie, "brother is sitting
in front of the door. He looks so white and has an apple
in his hand. I asked him to give me the apple but he
wouldn't answer me, and it made my flesh creep!" "Go
back out," said her mother, "and if he won't answer
you, you box his ears for him." And so Ann Marie went
out and said, "Brother, give me your apple," but he
said nothing and so she boxed his ears, and his head
fell off and she was horror-stricken and began to cry
and to scream and ran to her mother and said, "Oh,
Mother, I've hit my brother and knocked his head off,"

and cried and cried and could not stop. "Ann Marie," said the mother, "what have you done! But you just keep quiet and nobody will know. After all, it can't be helped now; we will stew him in a sour broth." And so the mother took the little boy and hacked him in pieces and put the pieces in the pot and stewed him in the sour broth. But Ann Marie stood by and cried and cried and the tears fell in the pot so that it didn't need any salt.

When the father came home he sat down to supper and said, "And where is my son?" And so the mother brought a big dish of black stew and Ann Marie cried and couldn't stop crying. And again the father said, "Where is my son?" "Oh," said the mother, "he's gone on a trip. He went to his mother's great-uncle and wants to stay there for a while." "What's he going to do there? And never even said goodbye to me!" "Oh, he wanted so much to go, he asked me if he could stay six weeks; they'll take good care of him there." "Ah," said the man, "why am I feeling so sad? It doesn't seem right, somehow. He might at least have come and said goodbye to me!" With that he began to eat and said,

"Ann Marie, what are you crying for? You'll see, your brother will be back." Then he said, "Ah, wife, what good food this is! Give me some more." And the more he ate the more he wanted, and said, "Give me more. You can't have any of it; it's as if all of this were for me." And he ate and ate, and threw the bones under the table, and finished it all up. But Ann Marie went to her chest of drawers and took her best silk scarf out of the bottom drawer and fetched every last little bone from under the table and tied them up in the silk cloth and carried them outside, weeping tears of blood. Then she laid them under the juniper tree in the green grass and as soon as she had laid them there she felt so much better and didn't cry any more. But the juniper began to stir and the branches kept opening out and coming back together again, just like someone who is really happy and goes like this with his hands. And then there was a sort of mist coming out of the tree and right in this mist it burned like fire and out of the fire flew this lovely bird that sang oh, so gloriously sweet and flew high into the air and when it was gone the juniper tree was just the way it had always been and

the cloth with the bones was gone. But Ann Marie felt so light of heart and so gay, just as if her brother were still alive. And so she went back into the house and was happy and sat down at the table and ate.

But the bird flew away and sat down on the roof of the goldsmith's house and began to sing:

> "My mother she butchered me,
>   My father he ate me,
>   My sister, little Ann Marie,
>   She gathered up the bones of me
>   And tied them in a silken cloth
>   To lay under the juniper.
>   Tweet twee, what a pretty bird am I!"

The goldsmith was sitting in his workshop, making a golden chain, and he heard the bird that sat on his roof and sang, and it seemed so beautiful to him. He got up and as he was walking across the doorstep he lost one of his slippers. But he kept walking right out into the middle of the street with one slipper and one stocking foot; he had his apron tied around his middle and in one hand he had the golden chain and in the other the pliers and the sun shone so brightly into the street. And he just stood there and looked at the bird. "Bird," said he, "how beautifully you sing! Sing that piece again." "No," said the bird, "the second time I don't sing for nothing. Give me the golden chain and I'll sing it again." "Here," said the goldsmith, "take the golden chain, now sing it again." And so the bird came and took the golden chain in its right claw and sat in front of the goldsmith and sang:

> "My mother she butchered me,
>   My father he ate me,
>   My sister, little Ann Marie,
>   She gathered up the bones of me
>   And tied them in a silken cloth
>   To lay under the juniper.
>   Tweet twee, what a pretty bird am I!"

And so the bird flew off to a cobbler's and sat down on the roof and sang:

> "My mother she butchered me,
>   My father he ate me,

The Juniper Tree

My sister, little Ann Marie,
She gathered up the bones of me
And tied them in a silken cloth
To lay under the juniper.
Tweet twee, what a pretty bird am I!"

The cobbler heard it and ran out of the door in his shirtsleeves and looked up to the roof and had to hold his hand over his eyes so the sun would not blind him. "Bird," said he, "how beautifully you sing!" And he called in through the door, "Wife, come out here a moment. There's a bird here, look at this bird! And how it can sing!" And he called his daughter and the children and the servants, the apprentice and the maid, and they all came into the street and saw the bird, how pretty it was, and it had such red feathers and green feathers and round the neck it was like pure gold and its eyes glittered in its head like stars. "Bird," said the cobbler, "sing me that piece again." "No," said the bird, "the second time I don't sing for nothing. You have to give me a present." "Wife," said the man, "go to the attic; up on the top shelf is a pair of red shoes, bring them down." And so the wife went up and got the shoes. "Here, bird," said the man, "now sing that piece again." And so the bird came and took the shoes in its left claw and flew back up to the roof and sang:

> "My mother she butchered me,
> My father he ate me,
> My sister, little Ann Marie,
> She gathered up the bones of me
> And tied them in a silken cloth
> To lay under the juniper.
> Tweet twee, what a pretty bird am I!"

And when it had finished singing, it flew away; it held the chain in its right claw and the shoes in its left, and flew far away to a mill and the mill went, "Clickety-clack, clickety-clack, clickety-clack." And in the door of the mill sat twenty of the miller's men hewing a new millstone and they chopped, "Chip-chop, chip-chop, chip-chop," and the mill went, "Clickety-clack, clickety-clack, clickety-clack." And so the bird went and sat on the linden tree that stood in front of the mill, and sang:

The Juniper Tree

"My mother she butchered me,"

and one of them stopped,

"My father he ate me,"

and two more stopped to listen,

"My sister, little Ann Marie,"

and four more stopped,

"She gathered up the bones of me
And tied them in a silken cloth,"

now there were only eight still chopping,

"To lay,"

now only five,

"under the juniper,"

now only one,

"Tweet twee, what a pretty bird am I!"

And so the last one stopped too and he had heard only
the last part. "Bird," said he, "how beautifully you sing!

327

I want to hear it too. Sing it again." "No," said the bird, "the second time I don't sing for nothing. Give me the millstone and I'll sing it again." "Yes," said he, "if it belonged to me alone, you could have it." "Yes," the others said, "if he sings again he can have it." And so the bird came down and the millers, all twenty of them, set the beam to and raised up the stone, "Heave-ho-hup, heave-ho-hup, heave-ho-hup." And the bird stuck its neck through the hole and put it on as if it were a collar and flew back into the tree and sang:

> "My mother she butchered me,
> My father he ate me,
> My sister, little Ann Marie,
> She gathered up the bones of me
> And tied them in a silken cloth
> To lay under the juniper.
> Tweet twee, what a pretty bird am I!"

And when it had finished singing, it spread its wings, and in the right claw it carried the chain, and the shoes in the left, and around the neck it wore the millstone, and flew all the way back to its father's house.

The Juniper Tree

Inside, the father, the mother, and Ann Marie were sitting at the table and the father said, "Ah, suddenly my heart feels so easy. Why do I feel so wonderfully good?" "No," said the mother, "I'm just so frightened, as if there was a great storm coming." But Ann Marie sat and cried and cried and right then the bird came flying along and as it sat down on the roof the father said, "How happy I'm feeling! And outside the sun is shining so brightly! It's just as if I were going to meet an old friend." "No," said the wife, "I'm so frightened! My teeth are chattering and it's as if I had fire in my veins." And she tore at her bodice to loosen it, but Ann Marie sat in a corner crying and held her plate in front of her eyes and cried so hard she was getting it wet and messy. And so the bird sat in the juniper tree and sang:

"My mother she butchered me"

And so then the mother stopped her ears up and squeezed her eyes shut and did not want to see or hear, but in her ears it roared like the wildest of storms and her eyes burned and twitched like lightning.

"My father he ate me"

"Ah, mother," said the man, "what a pretty bird and how sweetly it sings, and the sun so warm, and everything smells like cinnamon."

"My sister, little Ann Marie"

And Ann Marie laid her head on her knees and just kept crying and crying, but the man said, "I'm going outside, I must see the bird close up." "Don't go!" said the woman. "I feel as if the whole house were trembling and in flames." But the man went outside and looked at the bird:

"She gathered up the bones of me
And tied them in a silken cloth
To lay under the juniper.
Tweet twee, what a pretty bird am I!"

With this the bird let the golden chain fall, and it fell right around the man's neck and looked so well on him, and he went inside and he said, "Look at the pretty bird, what a pretty golden chain it gave me for a present, and how pretty it is to look at!" But the woman was so frightened she fell full length on the floor and the cap fell off her head. And still the bird sang.

"My mother she butchered me"

"I wish I were a thousand miles under the earth so that I wouldn't have to hear it."

"My father he ate me"

And the woman lay there as if she were dead.

"My sister, little Ann Marie"

"Ah," said Ann Marie, "I'm going out too to see if the bird has a present for me," and so she went out.

"She gathered up the bones of me
And tied them in a silken cloth,"

and here it threw the shoes down to her.

"To lay under the juniper.
Tweet twee, what a pretty bird am I!"

And she felt so lighthearted and gay. She put on the new red shoes and came dancing and skipping into the house. "Ah," said she, "I was so sad when I went outside, and now I feel so much better. What a wonderful bird it is! It gave me a pair of red shoes for a present." "No," said the woman and she jumped up and her hair stood straight on end like flaming fire. "It's as if the world were coming to an end. I'm going out and maybe I will feel better too." And as she came out of the door, crunch! the bird threw the millstone on her head and she was squashed. The father and Ann Marie heard it and came out. There was steam and flames and fire rising from the spot, and when they were gone, there stood the little brother and he took his father and Ann Marie by the hand and the three of them were so happy and went into the house and sat down at the table and ate their supper.

Printed by Pearl Pressman Liberty, Philadelphia
Bound by A. Horowitz and Son, Clifton, New Jersey
Designed by Atha Tehon and Maurice Sendak

DATE DUE
